Shooting Crocodiles

•

The distance was about a hundred yards, a fine range for the little rifle. Resting on his knee, he sighted low, under the gray object, and pulled the trigger twice. There were two *spats* so close together as to be barely distinguishable. The log of driftwood leaped into life.

"Whoop!" shouted Hal.

"It's a crocodile!" yelled George. "You hit—you hit! Will you listen to that?"

"Row hard, Pepe—pull!"

He bent to the oars, and the boat flew shoreward.

The huge crocodile, opening yard-long jaws, snapped them shut with loud cracks. Then he beat the bank with his tail. It was as limber as a willow, but he seemed unable to move his central parts, his thick bulk, where Ken had sent the two mushroom bullets. *Whack! Whack! Whack!* The sodden blows jarred pieces from the clay-bank above him. Each blow was powerful enough to have staved in the planking of a ship. All at once he lunged upward and, falling over backward, slid down his runway into a few inches of water, where he stuck.

KEN WARD
IN THE
JUNGLE

ZANE GREY

A TOM DOHERTY ASSOCIATES BOOK
NEW YORK

This is a work of fiction. All the characters and events portrayed in this book are either products of the author's imagination or are used fictitiously.

KEN WARD IN THE JUNGLE

All new material copyright © 1998 by Tom Doherty Associates, Inc.

A Forge Book
Published by Tom Doherty Associates, Inc.
175 Fifth Avenue
New York, NY 10010

Forge® is a registered trademark of Tom Doherty Associates, Inc.

ISBN: 0-812-58041-9

First Forge edition: July 1998

Printed in the United States of America

0 9 8 7 6 5 4 3 2 1

Contents

●

1. The Prize 1
2. The Home of the Tarpon.............................11
3. An Indian Boatman....................................20
4. At the Jungle River 28
5. The First Camp 36
6. Wilderness Life 44
7. Running the Rapids 56
8. The First Tiger-cat 69
9. In the White Water 79
10. Lost! 92
11. An Army of Snakes....................................101
12. Catching Strange Fish................................114
13. A Turkey-hunt 126
14. A Fight with a Jaguar 138
15. The Vicious Garrapatoes 148
16. Field Work of a Naturalist.........................154
17. A Mixed-up Tiger-hunt..............................161
18. Watching a Runway 172
19. Adventures with Crocodiles 181
20. Treed by Wild Pigs....................................196

CONTENTS

• • •

21. The Leaping Tarpon...................................206
22. Stricken Down.......................................220
23. Out of the Jungle..................................235

1

The Prize

●

"What a change from the Arizona desert!"

The words broke from the lips of Ken Ward as he leaned from the window of the train which was bearing his brother and himself over the plateau to Tampico in Tamaulipas, the southeastern state of Mexico. He had caught sight of a river leaping out between heavily wooded slopes and plunging down in the most beautiful waterfall he had ever seen.

"Look, Hal," he cried.

The first fall was a long white streak, ending in a dark pool; below came cascade after cascade, fall after fall, some wide, others narrow, and all white and green against the yellow rock. Then the train curved round a spur of the mountain, descended to a level, to be lost in a luxuriance of jungle growth.

1

KEN WARD IN THE JUNGLE

• • •

It was indeed a change for Ken Ward, young forester, pitcher of the varsity nine at school, and hunter of lions in the Arizona *cañons*. Here he was entering the jungle of the tropics. The rifles and the camp outfit on the seat beside his brother Hal and himself spoke of coming adventures. Before them lay an unknown wilderness—the semi-tropical jungle. And the future was to show that the mystery of the jungle was stranger even than their imaginings.

It was not love of adventure alone or interest in the strange new forest growths that had drawn Ken to the jungle. His uncle, the one who had gotten Ken letters from the Forestry Department at Washington, had been proud of Ken's Arizona achievements. This uncle was a member of the American Geographical Society and a fellow of the New York Museum of Natural History. He wanted Ken to try his hand at field work in the jungle of Mexico, and if that was successful, then to explore the ruined cities of wild Yucatan. If Ken made good as an explorer, his reward was to be a trip to Equatorial Africa after big game. And of course that trip meant an opportunity to see England and France, and, what meant more to Ken, a chance to see the great forests of Germany, where forestry had been carried on for three hundred years.

In spite of the fact that the inducement was irresistible, and that Ken's father was as proud and eager as Ken's uncle to have him make a name for himself, and that Hal would be allowed to go with him, Ken had hesitated. There was the responsibility for Hal and the absolute certainty that Hal could not keep out of mischief.

2

THE PRIZE

● ● ●

Still Ken simply could not have gone to Mexico leaving his brother at home broken-hearted.

At last the thing had been decided. It was Hal's ambition to be a naturalist and to collect specimens, and the uncle had held out possible recognition from the Smithsonian Institution at Washington. Perhaps he might find a new variety of some animal to which the scientists would attach his name. Then the lad was passionately eager to see Ken win that trip to Africa. There had been much study of maps and books of travel, science, and natural history. There had been the most careful instruction and equipment for semi-tropical camp life. The uncle had given Ken valuable lessons in map-drawing, in estimating distance, and in topography, and he had indicated any one of several rivers in the jungle belt of Mexico. Traversing one hundred miles of unknown jungle river, with intelligent observation and accurate reports, would win the prize for Ken Ward. Now the race was on. Would Ken win?

Presently the train crossed a bridge. Ken Ward had a brief glance at clear green water, at great cypress trees, gray and graceful with long, silvery, waving moss, and at the tangled, colorful banks. A water-fowl black as coal, with white-crested wings, skimmed the water in swift wild flight, to disappear up the shady river-lane. Then the train clattered on, and, a mile or more beyond the bridge, stopped at a station called Valles. In the distance could be seen the thatched palm-leaf huts and red-tiled roofs of a hamlet.

The boys got out to stretch their legs. The warm, sweet, balmy air was a new and novel thing to them.

3

● ● ●

They strolled up and down the gravel walk, watching the natives. Hal said he rather liked the looks of their brown bare feet and the thin cotton trousers and shirts, but he fancied the enormous sombreros were too heavy and unwieldy. Ken spoke to several pleasant-faced Mexicans, each of whom replied: "No sabe, Señor."

The ticket agent at the station was an American, and from the way he smiled and spoke Ken knew he was more than glad to see one of his own kind. So, after Ken had replied to many questions about the States, he began to ask some of his own.

"What's the name of the waterfall we passed?"

"Micas Falls," replied the agent.

"And the river?"

"It's called the Santa Rosa."

"Where does it go?"

The agent did not know, except that it disappeared in the jungle. Southward the country was wild. The villages were few and all along the railroad; and at Valles the river swung away to the southwest.

"But it must flow into the Panuco River," said Ken. He had studied maps of Mexico and had learned all that it was possible to learn before he undertook the journey.

"Why, yes, it must find the Panuco somewhere down over the mountain," answered the agent.

"Then there are rapids in this little river?" asked Ken, in growing interest.

"Well, I guess. It's all rapids."

"How far to Tampico by rail?" went on Ken.

4

THE PRIZE

● ● ●

"Something over a hundred miles."

"Any game in the jungle hereabouts—or along the Santa Rosa?" continued Ken.

The man laughed and laughed in such a way that Ken did not need his assertion that it was not safe to go into the jungle.

Whereupon Ken Ward became so thoughtful that he did not hear the talk that followed between the agent and Hal. The engine bell roused him into action, and with Hal he hurried back to their seats. And then the train sped on. But the beauty of Micas Falls and the wildness of the Santa Rosa remained with Ken. Where did that river go? How many waterfalls and rapids did it have? What teeming life must be along its rich banks! It haunted Ken. He wanted to learn the mystery of the jungle. There was the same longing which had gotten him into the wild adventures in Penetier Forest and the Grand Cañon country of Arizona. And all at once flashed over him the thought that here was the jungle river for him to explore.

"Why, that's the very thing," he said, thinking aloud.

"What's wrong with you," said Hal, "talking to yourself that way?"

Ken did not explain. The train clattered between green walls of jungle, and occasionally stopped at a station. But the thought of the jungle haunted him until the train arrived at Tampico.

Ken had the name of an American hotel, and that was all he knew about Tampico. The station was crowded with natives. Man after man accosted the boys, jab-

5

• • •

bering excitedly in Mexican. Some of these showed brass badges bearing a number and the word *Cargodore*.

"Hal, I believe these fellows are porters or baggage-men," said Ken. And he showed his trunk check to one of them. The fellow jerked it out of Ken's hand and ran off. The boys ran after him. They were relieved to see him enter a shed full of baggage. And they were amazed to see him kneel down and take their trunk on his back. It was a big trunk and heavy. The man was small and light.

"It'll smash him!" cried Hal.

But the little *cargodore* walked off with the trunk on his back. Then Ken and Hal saw other *cargodores* packing trunks. The boys kept close to their man and used their eyes with exceeding interest. The sun was setting, and the square, colored buildings looked as if they were in a picture of Spain.

"Look at the boats—canoes!" cried Hal, as they crossed a canal.

Ken saw long narrow canoes that had been hollowed out from straight tree trunks. They were of every size, and some of the paddles were enormous. Crowds of natives were jabbering and jostling each other at a rude wharf.

"Look back," called Hal, who seemed to have a hundred eyes.

Ken saw a wide, beautiful river, shining red in the sunset. Palm trees on the distant shore showed black against the horizon.

"Hal, that's the Panuco. What a river!"

THE PRIZE

● ● ●

"Makes the Susquehanna look like a creek," was Hal's comment.

The *cargodore* led the boys through a plaza, down a narrow street to the hotel. Here they were made to feel at home. The proprietor was a kindly American. The hotel was crowded, and many of the guests were Englishmen there for the tarpon fishing, with sportsmen from the States, and settlers coming in to take up new lands. It was pleasant for Ken and Hal to hear their own language once more. After dinner they sallied forth to see the town. But the narrow dark streets and the blanketed natives stealing silently along were not particularly inviting. The boys got no farther than the plaza, where they sat down on a bench. It was wholly different from any American town. Ken suspected that Hal was getting homesick, for the boy was quiet and inactive.

"I don't like this place," said Hal. "What'd you ever want to drag me way down here for?"

"Humph! Drag you? Say, you pestered the life out of me, and bothered Dad till he was mad, and worried mother sick to let you come on this trip."

Hal hung his head.

"Now, you're not going to show a streak of yellow?" asked Ken. He knew how to stir his brother.

Hal rose to the attack and scornfully repudiated the insinuation. Ken replied that they were in a new country and must not reach conclusions too hastily.

"I liked it back up there at the little village where we saw the green river and the big trees with the gray streamers on them," said Hal.

7

• • •

"Well, I liked that myself," rejoined Ken. "I'd like to go back there and put a boat in the river and come all the way here."

Ken had almost unconsciously expressed the thought that had been forming in his mind. Hal turned slowly and looked at his brother.

"Ken, that'd be great—that's what we came for!"

"I should say so," replied Ken.

"Well?" asked Hal, simply.

That question annoyed Ken. Had he not come south to go into the jungle? Had he come with any intention of shirking the danger of a wild trip? There was a subtle flattery in Hal's question.

"That Santa Rosa River runs through the jungle," went on Hal. "It flows into the Panuco somewhere. You know we figured out on the map that the Panuco's the only big river in this jungle. That's all we want to know. And, Ken, you know you're a born boatman. Why, look at the rapids we've shot on the Susquehanna. Remember that trip we came down the Juniata? The water was high, too. Ken, you can take a boat down that Santa Rosa!"

"By George! I believe I can," exclaimed Ken, and he thrilled at the thought.

"Ken, let's go. You'll win the prize, and I'll get specimens. Think what we'd have to tell Jim Williams and Dick Leslie when we go West next summer!"

"Oh, Hal, I know—but this idea of a trip seems too wild."

"Maybe it wouldn't be so wild."

In all fairness Ken could not deny this, so he kept silent.

THE PRIZE

● ● ●

"Ken, listen," went on Hal, and now he was quite cool. "If we'd promised the governor not to take a wild trip, I wouldn't say another word. But we're absolutely free."

"That's why we ought to be more careful. Dad trusts me."

"He trusts you because he knows you can take care of yourself, and me, too. You're a wonder, Ken. Why, if you once made up your mind, you'd make that Santa Rosa River look like a canal."

Ken began to fear that he would not be proof against the haunting call of that jungle river and the flattering persuasion of his brother and the ever-present ambition to show his uncle what he could do.

"Hal, if I didn't have you with me I'd already have made up my mind to tackle this river."

That appeared to insult Hal.

"All I've got to say is I'd be a help to you—not a drag," he said, with some warmth.

"You're always a help, Hal. I can't say anything against your willingness. But you know your weakness. By George! you made trouble enough for me in Arizona. On a trip such as this you'd drive me crazy."

"Ken, I won't make any rash promises. I don't want to queer myself with you. But I'm all right."

"Look here, Hal, let's wait. We've only got to Tampico. Maybe such a trip is impracticable—impossible. Let's find out more about the country."

Hal appeared to take this in good spirit. The boys returned to the hotel and went to bed. Hal promptly fell asleep. But Ken Ward lay awake a long time thinking of the green Santa Rosa, with its magnificent moss-festooned cypresses. And when he did go to sleep it was to dream of the beautiful water-fowl with the white-crested wings, and he was following it on its wild flight down the dark, mysterious river-trail into the jungle.

2

The Home of the Tarpon

•

Hal's homesickness might never have been in evidence at all, to judge from the way the boy, awakening at dawn, began to talk about the Santa Rosa trip.

"Well," said Ken, as he rolled out of bed, "I guess we're in for it."

"Ken, will we go?" asked Hal, eagerly.

"I'm on the fence."

"But you're leaning on the jungle side?"

"Yes, kid—I'm slipping."

Hal opened his lips to let out a regular Hiram Bent yell, when Ken clapped a hand over his mouth.

"Hold on—we're in the hotel yet."

It took the brothers long to dress, because they could not keep away from the window. The sun was rising in rosy glory over misty lagoons. Clouds of creamy mist rolled above the broad Panuco. Wild ducks were flying

● ● ●

low. The tiled roofs of the stone houses gleamed brightly, and the palm trees glistened with dew. The soft breeze that blew in was warm, sweet, and fragrant.

After breakfast the boys went out to the front and found the hotel lobby full of fishermen and their native boatmen. It was an interesting sight, as well as a surprise, for Ken and Hal did not know that Tampico was as famous for fishing as it was for hunting. The huge rods and reels amazed them.

"What kind of fish do these fellows fish for?" asked Hal.

Ken was well enough acquainted with sport to know something about tarpon, but he had never seen one of the great silver fish. And he was speechless when Hal led him into a room upon the walls of which were mounted specimens of tarpon from six to seven feet in length and half as wide as a door.

"Say, Ken! We've come to the right place. Those fishermen are all going out to fish for such whales as these here."

"Hal, we never saw a big fish before," said Ken. "And before we leave Tampico we'll know what it means to hook tarpon."

"I'm with you," replied Hal, gazing doubtfully and wonderingly at a fish almost twice as big as himself.

Then Ken, being a practical student of fishing, as of other kinds of sport, began to stroll round the lobby with an intent to learn. He closely scrutinized the tackle. And he found that the bait used was a white mullet six to ten inches long, a little fish which resembled the chub. Ken did not like the long, cruel gaff which seemed a necessary adjunct to each outfit of tackle, and

● ● ●

he vowed that in his fishing for tarpon he would dispense with it.

Ken was not backward about asking questions, and he learned that Tampico, during the winter months, was a rendezvous for sportsmen from all over the world. For the most part, they came to catch the leaping tarpon; the shooting along the Panuco, however, was as well worthwhile as the fishing. But Ken could not learn anything about the Santa Rosa River. The *tierra caliente*, or hot belt, along the curve of the Gulf was intersected by small streams, many of them unknown and unnamed. The Panuco swung round to the west and had its source somewhere up in the mountains. Ken decided that the Santa Rosa was one of its headwaters. Valles lay up on the first swell of higher ground, and was distant from Tampico some six hours by train. So, reckoning with the meandering course of jungle streams, Ken calculated he would have something like one hundred and seventy-five miles to travel by water from Valles to Tampico. There were Indian huts strung along the Panuco River, and fifty miles inland a village named Panuco. What lay between Panuco and Valles, up over the wild steppes of that jungle, Ken Ward could only conjecture.

Presently he came upon Hal in conversation with an American boy, who at once volunteered to show them around. So they set out, and were soon becoming well acquainted. Their guide said he was from Kansas, had been working in the railroad offices for two years, and was now taking a vacation. His name was George Alling. Under his guidance the boys spent several interesting hours going about the city. During this walk Hal

13

showed his first tendency to revert to his natural bent of mind. Not for long could Hal Ward exist without making trouble for something. In this case it was buzzards, of which the streets of Tampico were full. In fact, George explained, the buzzards were the only street-cleaning department in the town. They were as tame as tame turkeys, and Hal could not resist the desire to chase them. And he could be made to stop only after a white-helmeted officer had threatened him. George explained further that although Tampico had no game laws it protected these buzzard-scavengers of the streets.

The market-house at the canal wharf was one place where Ken thought Hal would forget himself in the bustle and din and color. All was so strange and new. Indeed, for a time Hal appeared to be absorbed in his surroundings, but when he came to a stall where a man had parrots and racoons and small deer, and three little yellow, black-spotted tiger-cats, as George called them, then once more Ken had to take Hal in tow. Outside along the wharf were moored a hundred or more canoes of manifold variety. All had been hewn from solid tree trunks. Some were long, slender, graceful, pretty to look at, and easy to handle in shallow lagoons, but Ken thought them too heavy and cumbersome for fast water. Happening just then to remember Micas Falls, Ken had a momentary chill and a check to his enthusiasm for the jungle trip. What if he encountered, in coming down the Santa Rosa, some such series of cascades as those which made Micas Falls!

It was about noon when George led the boys out to the banks of the broad Panuco. Both Hal and Ken were

● ● ●

suffering from the heat. They had removed their coats, and were now very glad to rest in the shade.

"This is a nice cool day," said George, and he looked cool.

"We've got on our heavy clothes, and this tropic sun is new to us," replied Ken. "Say, Hal—"

A crash in the water near the shore interrupted Ken.

"Was that a rhinoceros?" inquired Hal.

"Savalo," said George.

"What's that?"

"Silver king. A tarpon. Look around and you'll see one break water. There are some fishermen trolling downstream. Watch. Maybe one will hook a fish presently. Then you'll see some jumping."

It was cool in the shade, as the brothers soon discovered, and they spent a delightful hour watching the river and the wild fowl and the tarpon. Ken and Hal were always lucky. Things happened for their benefit and pleasure. Not only did they see many tarpon swirl like bars of silver on the water, but a fisherman hooked one of the great fish not fifty yards from where the boys sat. And they held their breath, and with starting eyes watched the marvelous leaps and dashes of the tarpon till, as he shot up in a last mighty effort, wagging his head, slapping his huge gills, and flinging the hook like a bullet, he plunged back free.

"Nine out of ten get away," remarked George.

"Did you ever catch one?" asked Hal.

"Sure."

"Hal, I've got to have some of this fishing," said Ken. "But if we start at it now—would we ever get that jungle trip?"

● ● ●

"Oh, Ken, you've made up your mind to go!" exclaimed Hal, in glee.

"No, I haven't," protested Ken.

"Yes, you have," declared Hal. "I know you." And the whoop that he had suppressed in the hotel he now let out with good measure.

Naturally George was interested, and at his inquiry Ken told him the idea for the Santa Rosa trip.

"Take me along," said George. There was a note of American spirit in his voice, a laugh on his lips, and a flash in his eyes that made Ken look at him attentively. He was a slim youth, not much Hal's senior, and Ken thought if ever a boy had been fashioned to be a boon comrade of Hal Ward this George Alling was the boy.

"What do you think of the trip?" inquired Ken, curiously.

"Fine. We'll have some fun. We'll get a boat and mozo—"

"What's a mozo?"

"A native boatman."

"That's a good idea. I hadn't thought of a boatman to help row. But the boat is the particular thing. I wouldn't risk a trip in one of those canoes."

"Come on, I'll find a boat," said George.

And before he knew it George and Hal were leading him back from the river. George led him down narrow lanes, between painted stone houses and iron-barred windows, till they reached the canal. They entered a yard where buzzards, goats, and razorback pigs were contesting over the scavenger rights. George went into a boat-house and pointed out a long, light, wide skiff with a flat bottom. Ken did not need George's praise, or

16

● ● ●

the shining light in Hal's eyes, or the boat-keeper's importunities to make him eager to try this particular boat. Ken Ward knew a boat when he saw one. He jumped in, shoved it out, rowed up the canal, pulled and turned, backed water, and tried every stroke he knew. Then he rested on the oars and whistled. Hal's shout of delight made him stop whistling. Those two boys would have him started on the trip if he did not look sharp.

"It's a dandy boat," said Ken.

"Only a peso a day, Ken," went on Hal. "One dollar Mex—fifty cents in our money. Quick, Ken, hire it before somebody else gets it."

"Sure I'll hire the boat," replied Ken, "but Hal, it's not for that Santa Rosa trip. We'll have to forget that."

"Forget your grandmother!" cried Hal. And then it was plain that he tried valiantly to control himself, to hide his joy, to pretend to agree with Ken's ultimatum.

Ken had a feeling that his brother knew him perfectly, and he was divided between anger and amusement. They returned to the hotel and lounged in the lobby. The proprietor was talking with some Americans, and as he now appeared to be at leisure he introduced the brothers and made himself agreeable. Moreover, he knew George Alling well. They began to chat, and Ken was considerably annoyed to hear George calmly state that he and his new-found friends intended to send a boat up to Valles and come down an unknown jungle river.

The proprietor laughed, and, though the laugh was not unpleasant, somehow it nettled Ken Ward.

"Why not go?" he asked, quietly, and he looked at the hotel man.

● ● ●

"My boy, you can't undertake any trip like that."

"Why not?" persisted Ken. "Is there any law here to prevent our going into the jungle?"

"There's no law. No one could stop you. But, my lad, what's the sense of taking such a fool trip? The river here is full of tarpon right now. There are millions of ducks and geese on the lagoons. You can shoot deer and wild turkey right on the edge of town. If you want tiger and javelin, go out to one of the ranches where they have dogs to hunt with, where you'll have a chance for your life. These tigers and boars will kill a man. There's all the sport anyone wants right close to Tampico."

"I don't see how all that makes a reason why we shouldn't come down the Santa Rosa," replied Ken. "We want to explore—map the river."

The hotel man seemed nettled in return.

"You're only kids. It'd be crazy to start out on that wild trip."

It was on Ken's lips to mention a few of the adventures which he believed justly gave him a right to have pride and confidence in his ability. But he forbore.

"It's a fool trip," continued the proprietor. "You don't know this river. You don't know where you'll come out. It's wild up in that jungle. I've hunted up at Valles, and no native I ever met would go a mile from the village. If you take a mozo, he'll get soaked with canya. He'll stick a knife in you or run off and leave you when you most need help. Nobody ever explored that river. It'll likely be full of swamps, sand-bars, bogs. You'd get fever. Then the crocodiles, the boars, the bats, the snakes, the tigers! Why, if you could face these you'd still have

18

● ● ●

the ticks—the worst of all. The ticks would drive men crazy, let alone boys. It's no undertaking for a boy."

The mention of all these dangers would have tipped the balance for Ken in favor of the Santa Rosa trip, even if the hint of his callowness had not roused his spirit.

"Thank you. I'm sure you mean kindly," said Ken. "But I'm going to Valles and I'll come down that jungle river."

3

An Indian Boatman

●

The moment the decision was made Ken felt both sorry and glad. He got the excited boys outside away from the critical and anxious proprietor. And Ken decided it was incumbent upon him to adopt a serious and responsible manner, which he was far from feeling. So he tried to be as cool as Hiram Bent, with a fatherly interest in the two wild boys who were to accompany him down the Santa Rosa.

"Now, George, steer us around till we find a mozo," said Ken. "Then we'll buy an outfit and get started on this trip before you can say Jack Robinson."

All the *mozos* the boys interviewed were eager to get work; however, when made acquainted with the nature of the trip they refused point blank.

"Tigre!" exclaimed one.

AN INDIAN BOATMAN

• • •

"Javelin!" exclaimed another.

The big spotted jaguar of the jungle and the wild boar, or peccary, were held in much dread by the natives.

"These natives will climb a tree at sight of a tiger or pig," said George. "For my part I'm afraid of the garrapatoes and the pinilius."

"What're they?" asked Hal.

"Ticks—jungle ticks. Just wait till you make their acquaintance."

Finally the boys met a *mozo* named Pepe, who had often rowed a boat for George. Pepe looked sadly in need of a job; still he did not ask for it. George said that Pepe had been one of the best boatmen on the river until *canya*, the fiery white liquor to which the natives were addicted, had ruined his reputation. Pepe wore an old sombrero, a cotton shirt and sash, and ragged trousers. He was barefooted. Ken noted the set of his muscular neck, his brawny shoulders and arms, and appreciated the years of rowing that had developed them. But Pepe's haggard face, deadened eyes, and listless manner gave Ken pause. Still, Ken reflected, there was never any telling what a man might do, if approached right. Pepe's dejection excited Ken's sympathy. So Ken clapped him on the shoulder, and, with George acting as interpreter, offered Pepe work for several weeks at three pesos a day. That was more than treble the *mozo's* wage. Pepe nearly fell off the canal bridge, where he was sitting, and a light as warm and bright as sunshine flashed into his face.

● ● ●

"Si, Señor—Si, Señor," he began to jabber, and waved his brown hands.

Ken suspected that Pepe needed a job and a little kind treatment. He was sure of it when George said Pepe's wife and children were in want. Somehow Ken conceived a liking for Pepe, and believed he could trust him. He thought he knew how to deal with poor Pepe. So he gave him money, told him to get a change of clothes and a pair of shoes and to come to the hotel the next day.

"He'll spend the money for canya, and not show up tomorrow," said George.

"I don't know anything about your natives, but that fellow will come," declared Ken.

It appeared that the whole American colony in Tampico had been acquainted with Ken Ward's project, and made a business to waylay the boys at each corner. They called the trip a wild-goose chase. They declared it was a dime-novel idea, and could hardly take Ken seriously. They mingled astonishment with amusement and concern. They advised Ken not to go, and declared they would not let him go. Over and over again the boys were assured of the peril from ticks, bats, boars, crocodiles, snakes, tigers, and fevers.

"That's what I'm taking the trip for," snapped Ken, driven to desperation by all this nagging.

"Well, young man, I admire your nerve," concluded the hotel man. "If you're determined to go, we can't stop you. And there's some things we would like you to find out for us. How far do tarpon run up the Panuco River? Do they spawn up there? How big are the new-born fish? I'll furnish you with tackle and preserved mullet for bait. We've always wondered about how far tarpon go up into fresh water. Keep your eye open for signs of oil. Also look at the timber. And be sure to make a map of the river."

When it came to getting the boat shipped the boys met with more obstacles. But for the friendly offices of a Texan, an employee of the railroad, they would never have been able to convince the native shipping agent that a boat was merchandise. The Texan arranged the matter and got Ken a freight bill. He took an entirely different view of Ken's enterprise, compared with that of other Americans, and in a cool, drawling voice, which somehow reminded Ken of Jim Williams, he said:

"Shore you-all will have the time of your lives. I worked at Valles for a year. That jungle is full of game. I killed three big tigers. You-all want to look out for those big yellow devils. One in every three will jump for a man. There's nothing but shoot, then. And the wild pigs are bad. They put me up a tree more than once. I don't know much about the Santa Rosa. Its source is above Micas Falls. Never heard where it goes. I know it's full of crocodiles and rapids. Never saw a boat or a canoe at Valles. And say—there are big black snakes in the jungle. Look out for them, too. Shore you-all have sport a-comin'."

Ken thanked the Texan, and as he went on up-street, for all his sober thoughtfulness, he was as eager as Hal or George. However, his position as their guardian would not permit any show of extravagant enthusiasm.

KEN WARD IN THE JUNGLE

● ● ●

Ken bought blankets, cooking utensils, and supplies for three weeks. There was not such a thing as a tent in Tampico. The best the boys could get for a shelter was a long strip of canvas nine feet wide.

"That'll keep off the wet," said Ken, "but it won't keep out the mosquitoes and things."

"Couldn't keep 'em out if we had six tents," replied George.

The remainder of that day the boys were busy packing the outfit.

Pepe presented himself at the hotel next morning an entirely different person. He was clean-shaven and no longer disheveled. He wore a new sombrero, a white cotton shirt, a red sash, and blue trousers. He carried a small bundle, a pair of shoes, and a long *machete*. The dignity with which he approached before all the other *mozos* was not lost upon Ken Ward. A sharp scrutiny satisfied him that Pepe had not been drinking. Ken gave him several errands to do. Then he ordered the outfit taken to the station in Pepe's charge.

The boys went down early in the afternoon. It was the time when the *mozos* were returning from the day's tarpon fishing on the river, and they, with the *cargodores*, streamed to and fro on the platform. Pepe was there standing guard over Ken's outfit. He had lost his fame among his old associates and for long had been an outsider. Here he was in charge of a pile of fine guns, fishing-tackle, baggage, and supplies—a collection representing a fortune to him and his simple class. He had been trusted with it. It was under his eye. All his old associates passed by to see him there.

AN INDIAN BOATMAN
● ● ●

That was a great time for Pepe. He looked bright, alert, and supremely happy. It would have fared ill with thieves or loafers who would have made themselves free with any of the articles under his watchful eye.

The train pulled out of Tampico at five o'clock, and Hal's "We're off!" was expressive.

The railroad lay along the riverbank, and the broad Panuco was rippling with the incoming tide. If Ken and Hal had not already found George to be invaluable as a companion in this strange country, they would have discovered it then. For George could translate Pepe's talk, and explain much that otherwise would have been dark to the brothers. Wild ducks dotted the green surface, and spurts showed where playful *ravalo* were breaking water. Great green-backed tarpon rolled their silver sides against the little waves. White cranes and blue herons stood like statues upon the reedy bars. Low down over the opposite bank of the river a long line of wild geese winged its way toward a shimmering lagoon. And against the gold and crimson of the sunset sky a flight of wild fowl stood out in bold black relief. The train crossed the Tamesi River and began to crawl away from the Panuco. On the right, wide marshes, gleaming purple in the darkening light, led the eye far beyond to endless pale lagoons. Birds of many kinds skimmed the weedy flats. George pointed out a flock of aigrets, the beautiful wild fowl with the priceless plumes. Then there was a string of pink flamingoes, tall, grotesque, wading along with waddling stride, feeding with heads under water.

● ● ●

"Great!" exclaimed Ken Ward.

"It's all so different from Arizona," said Hal.

At Tamos, twelve miles out of Tampico, the train entered the jungle. Thereafter the boys could see nothing but the impenetrable green walls that lined the track. At dusk the train reached a station called Las Palmas, and then began to ascend the first step of the mountain. The ascent was steep, and, when it was accomplished, Ken looked down and decided that step of the mountain was between two and three thousand feet high. The moon was in its first quarter, and Ken, studying this tropical moon, found it large, radiant, and a wonderful green-gold. It shed a soft luminous glow down upon the sleeping, tangled web of jungle. It was new and strange to Ken, so vastly different from barren desert or iron-ribbed *cañon*, and it thrilled him with nameless charm.

The train once more entered jungle walls, and as the boys could not see anything out of the windows they lay back in their seats and waited for the ride to end. They were due at Valles at ten o'clock, and the impatient Hal complained that they would never get there. At length a sharp whistle from the engine caused Pepe to turn to the boys with a smile.

"Valles," he said.

With rattle and clank the train came to a halt. Ken sent George and Pepe out, and he and Hal hurriedly handed the luggage through the open window. When the last piece had been passed into Pepe's big hands the boys made a rush for the door, and jumped off as the train started.

AN INDIAN BOATMAN

● ● ●

"Say, but it's dark," said Hal.

As the train with its lights passed out of sight Ken found himself in what seemed a pitchy blackness. He could not see the boys. And he felt a little cold sinking of his heart at the thought of such black nights on an unknown jungle river.

4

At the Jungle River

•

Presently, as Ken's eyes became accustomed to the change, the darkness gave place to pale moonlight. A crowd of chattering natives, with wide sombreros on their heads and blankets over their shoulders, moved round the little stone station. Visitors were rare in Valles, as was manifested by the curiosity aroused by the boys and the pile of luggage.

"Ask Pepe to find some kind of lodging for the night," said Ken to George.

Pepe began to question the natives, and soon was lost in the crowd. Awhile after, as Ken was making up his mind they might have to camp on the station platform, a queer low bus drawn by six little mules creaked up. Pepe jumped off the seat beside the driver, and began to stow the luggage away in the bus. Then the boys piled in behind, and were soon bowling along

● ● ●

a white moonlit road. The soft voices of natives greeted their passing.

Valles appeared to be about a mile from the station, and as they entered the village Ken made out rows of thatched huts, and here and there a more pretentious habitation of stone. At length the driver halted before a rambling house, partly stone and partly thatch. There were no lights; in fact, Ken did not see a light in the village. George told the boys to take what luggage each could carry and follow the guide. Inside the house it was as dark as a dungeon. The boys bumped into things and fell over each other trying to keep close to the bare-footed and mysterious guide. Finally they climbed to a kind of loft, where the moonlight streamed in at the open sides.

"What do you think of this?" panted Hal, who had struggled with a heavy load of luggage. Pepe and the guide went down to fetch up the remainder of the outfit. Ken thought it best to stand still until he knew just where he was. But Hal and George began moving about in the loft. It was very large and gloomy, and seemed open, yet full of objects. Hal jostled into something which creaked and fell with a crash. Then followed a yell, the jabbering of a frightened native, and a scuffling about.

"Hal, what'd you do?" called Ken, severely.

"You can search me," replied Hal Ward. "One thing—I busted my shin."

"He knocked over a bed with someone sleeping in it," said George.

Pepe arrived in the loft then and soon soothed the injured feelings of the native who had been so rudely dis-

turbed. He then led the boys to their cots, which were
no more than heavy strips of canvas stretched over tall
frameworks. They appeared to be enormously high for
beds. Ken's was as high as his head, and Ken was tall
for his age.

"Say, I'll never get up into this thing," burst out Hal.
"These people must be afraid to sleep near the floor.
George, why are these cots so high?"

"I reckon to keep the pigs and dogs and all that from
sleeping with the natives," answered George. "Besides,
the higher you sleep in Mexico the farther you get from
creeping, crawling things."

Ken had been of half a mind to sleep on the floor, but
George's remark had persuaded him to risk the lofty
cot. It was most awkward to climb into. Ken tried several times without success, and once he just escaped a
fall. By dint of muscle and a good vault he finally
landed in the center of his canvas. From there he listened to his more unfortunate comrades. Pepe got into
his without much difficulty. George, however, in climbing up, on about the fifth attempt swung over too hard
and rolled off on the other side. The thump he made
when he dropped jarred the whole loft. From the various growls out of the darkness it developed that the loft
was full of sleepers, who were not pleased at this inva-
sion. Then Hal's cot collapsed, and went down with a
crash. And Hal sat on the flattened thing and laughed.

"Mucho malo," Pepe said, and he laughed, too. Then
he had to get out and put up Hal's trestle bed. Hal once
again went to climbing up the framework, and this time,
with Pepe's aid, managed to surmount it.

AT THE JUNGLE RIVER

● ● ●

"George, what does Pepe mean by 'mucho malo'?" asked Hal.

"Bad—very much bad," replied George.

"Nix—tell him nix. This is fine," said Hal.

"Boys, if you don't want to sleep yourselves, shut up so the rest of us can," ordered Ken.

He liked the sense of humor and the good fighting spirit of the boys, and fancied they were the best attributes in comrades on a wild trip. For a long time he heard a kind of shuddering sound, which he imagined was Hal's cot quivering as the boy laughed. Then absolute quiet prevailed, the boys slept, and Ken felt himself drifting.

When he awakened the sun was shining through the holes in the thatched roof. Pepe was up, and the other native sleepers were gone. Ken and the boys descended from their perches without any tumbles, had a breakfast that was palatable—although even George could not name what they ate—and then were ready for the day.

Valles consisted of a few stone houses and many thatched huts of bamboo and palm. There was only one street, and it was full of pigs, dogs, and buzzards. The inhabitants manifested a kindly interest and curiosity, which changed to consternation when they learned of the boys' project. Pepe questioned many natives, and all he could learn about the Santa Rosa was that there was an impassable waterfall some few kilometers below Valles. Ken gritted his teeth and said they would have to get past it. Pepe did not encounter a man who had ever heard of the headwaters of the Panuco River. There were only a few fields under cultivation around Valles, and they were enclosed by impenetrable jungle. It

31

seemed useless to try to find out anything about the river. But Pepe's advisers in the village told enough about *tigre* and *javelin* to make Hal's hair stand on end and George turn pale and Ken himself wish they had not come. It all gave Ken both a thrill and a shock.

There was not much conversation among the boys on the drive back to the station. However, sight of the boat, which had come by freight, stirred Ken with renewed spirit, and through him that was communicated to the others.

The hardest task, so far, developed in the matter of transporting the boat and supplies out to the river. Ken had hoped to get a hand-car and haul the outfit on the track down to where the bridge crossed the Santa Rosa. But there was no hand-car. Then came the staggering information that there was no wagon which would carry the boat, and then worse still the fact that there was no road. This discouraged Ken; nevertheless, he had not the least idea of giving up. He sent Pepe out to tell the natives there must be some way to get the outfit to the river.

Finally Pepe found a fellow who had a cart. This fellow claimed he knew a trail that went to a point from which it would be easy to carry the boat to the river. Ken had Pepe hire the man at once.

"Bring on your old cart," said the irrepressible Hal.

That cart turned out to be a remarkable vehicle. It consisted of a narrow body between enormously high wheels. A trio of little mules was hitched to it. The driver willingly agreed to haul the boat and outfit for one *peso*, but when he drove up to the platform to be surrounded by neighbors, he suddenly discovered that

● ● ●

he could not possibly accommodate the boys. Patiently Pepe tried to persuade him. No, the thing was impossible. He made no excuses, but he looked mysterious.

"George, tell Pepe to offer him five pesos," said Ken.

Pepe came out bluntly with the inducement, and the driver began to sweat. From the look of his eyes Ken fancied he had not earned so much money in a year. Still he was cunning, and his whispering neighbors lent him support. He had the only cart in the village, and evidently it seemed that fortune had come to knock at least once at his door. He shook his head.

Ken held up both hands with fingers spread. "Ten pesos," he said.

The driver, like a crazy man, began to jabber his consent.

The boys lifted the boat upon the cart, and tied it fast in front so that the stern would not sag. Then they packed the rest of the outfit inside.

Ken was surprised to see how easily the little mules trotted off with such a big load. At the edge of the jungle he looked back toward the station. The motley crowd of natives were watching, making excited gestures, and all talking at once. The driver drove onto a narrow trail, which closed behind him. Pepe led on foot, brushing aside the thick foliage. Ken drew a breath of relief as he passed into the cool shade. The sun was very hot. Hal and George brought up the rear, talking fast.

The trail was lined and overgrown with slender trees, standing very close, making dense shade. Many birds, some of beautiful coloring, flitted in the branches. In about an hour the driver entered a little clearing where there were several thatched huts. Ken heard the puffing of an engine, and, looking through the trees, he saw the railroad and knew they had arrived at the pumping station and the bridge over the Santa Rosa.

Pepe lost no time in rounding up six natives to carry the boat. They did not seem anxious to oblige Pepe, although they plainly wanted the money he offered. The trouble was the boat, at which they looked askance. As in the case with the driver, however, the weight and clinking of added silver overcame their reluctance. They easily lifted the boat upon their shoulders. And as they entered the trail, making a strange procession in the close-bordering foliage, they encountered two natives, who jumped and ran, yelling: "La diable! La diable!"

"What ails those gazabos?" asked Hal.

"They're scared," replied George. "They thought the boat was the devil."

If Ken needed any more than had already come to him about the wildness of the Santa Rosa, he had it in the frightened cries and bewilderment of these natives. They had never seen a boat. The Santa Rosa was a beautiful wild river upon which boats were unknown. Ken had not hoped for so much. And now that the die was cast he faced the trip with tingling gladness.

"George and Hal, you stay behind to watch the outfit. Pepe and I will carry what we can and follow the boat. I'll send back after you," said Ken.

Then as he followed Pepe and the natives down the trail there was a deep satisfaction within him. He heard the soft rush of water over stones and the mourning of turtle-doves. He rounded a little hill to come abruptly upon the dense green mass of river foliage. Giant

● ● ●

cypress trees, bearded with gray moss, fringed the banks. Through the dark green of leaves Ken caught sight of light green water. Birds rose all about him. There were rustlings in the thick underbrush and the whir of ducks. The natives penetrated the dark shade and came out to an open, grassy point.

The Santa Rosa, glistening, green, swift, murmured at Ken's feet. The natives dropped the boat into the water, and with Pepe went back for the rest of the outfit. Ken looked up the shady lane of the river and thought of the moment when he had crossed the bridge in the train. Then, as much as he had longed to be there, he had not dared to hope it. And here he was! How strange it was, just then, to see a large black duck with white-crested wings sweep by as swift as the wind! Ken had seen that wild fowl, or one of his kind, and it had haunted him.

5

The First Camp

●

In less than an hour all the outfit had been carried down to the river, and the boys sat in the shade, cooling off, happily conscious that they had made an auspicious start.

It took Ken only a moment to decide to make camp there and the next day try to reach Micas Falls. The mountains appeared close at hand, and were so lofty that, early in the afternoon as it was, the westering sun hung over the blue summits. The notch where the Santa Rosa cut through the range stood out clear, and at most it was not more than eighteen miles distant. So Ken planned to spend a day pulling up the river, and then to turn for the downstream trip.

"Come, boys, let's make camp," said Ken.

He sent Pepe with his long *machete* into the brush to cut firewood. Hal he set to making a stone fireplace,

THE FIRST CAMP

• • •

which work the boy rather prided himself upon doing well. Ken got George to help him to put up the strip of canvas. They stretched a rope between two trees, threw the canvas over it, and pegged down the ends.

"Say, how're we going to sleep?" inquired Hal, suddenly.

"Sleep? Why, on our backs, of course," retorted Ken, who could read Hal's mind.

"If we don't have some hot old times keeping things out of this tent, I'm a lobster," said George, dubiously. "I'm going to sleep in the middle."

"You're a brave boy, George," replied Ken.

"Me for between Ken and Pepe," added Hal.

"And you're twice as brave," said Ken. "I dare say Pepe and I will be able to keep things from getting at you."

Just as Pepe came into camp staggering under a load of wood, a flock of russet-colored ducks swung round the bend. They alighted near the shore at a point opposite the camp. The way George and Hal made headers into the pile of luggage for their guns gave Ken an inkling of what he might expect from these lads. He groaned, and then he laughed. George came up out of the luggage first, and he had a .22-caliber rifle, which he quickly loaded and fired into the flock. He crippled one; the others flew upstream. Then George began to waste shells trying to kill the crippled duck. Hal got into action with his .22. They bounced bullets off the water all around the duck, but they could not hit it.

Pepe grew as excited as the boys, and he jumped into the boat and with a long stick began to pole out into the

37

stream. Ken had to caution George and Hal to lower their guns and not shoot Pepe. Below camp and just under the bridge the water ran into a shallow rift. The duck got onto the current and went round the bend, with Pepe poling in pursuit and George and Hal yelling along the shore. When they returned a little later, they had the duck, which was of an unknown species to Ken. Pepe had fallen overboard; George was wet to his knees; and, though Hal did not show any marks of undue exertion, his eyes would have enlightened any beholder. The fact was that they were glowing with the excitement of the chase. It amused Ken. He felt that he had to try to stifle his own enthusiasm. There had to be one old head in the party. But if he did have qualms over the possibilities of the boys to worry him with their probable escapades, he still felt happy at their boundless life and spirit.

It was about the middle of the afternoon, and the heat had become intense. Ken realized it doubly when he saw Pepe favoring the shade. George and Hal were hot, but they appeared to be too supremely satisfied with their surroundings to care about that.

During this hot spell, which lasted from three o'clock until five, there was a quiet and a lack of life around camp that surprised Ken. It was slumberland; even the insects seemed drowsy. Not a duck and scarcely a bird passed by. Ken heard the mourning of turtle-doves, and was at once struck with the singular deep, full tone. Several trains crossed the bridge, and at intervals the engine at the pumping-tank puffed and chugged. From time to time a native walked out upon the bridge to stare long and curiously at the camp.

THE FIRST CAMP

• • •

When the sun set behind the mountain a hard breeze swept down the river. Ken did not know what to make of it, and at first thought there was going to be a storm. Pepe explained that the wind blew that way every day after sunset. For a while it tossed the willows, and waved the Spaniard's-beard upon the cypresses. Then as suddenly as it had come it died away, taking the heat with it.

Whereupon the boys began to get supper.

"George, do you know anything about this water?" asked Ken. "Is it safe?"

George supposed it was all right, but he did not know. The matter of water had bothered Ken more than any other thing in consideration of the trip. This river-water was cool and clear; it apparently was safe. But Ken decided not to take any chances, and to boil all the water used. All at once George yelled, "Canvasbacks!" and made a dive for his gun. Ken saw a flock of ducks swiftly winging flight upstream.

"Hold on, George. Don't shoot," called Ken. "Let's go a little slow at the start."

George appeared to be disappointed, though he promptly obeyed.

Then the boys had supper, finding the russet duck much to their taste. Ken made a note of Pepe's capacity, and was glad there were prospects of plenty of meat. While they were eating, a group of natives gathered on the bridge. Ken would not have liked to interpret their opinion of his party from their actions.

Night came on almost before the boys were ready for it. They replenished the camp-fire, and sat around it, looking into the red blaze and then out into the flicker-

39

• • •

ing shadows. Ken thought the time propitious for a little lecture he had to give the boys, and he remembered how old Hiram Bent had talked to him and Hal that first night down under the great black rim-wall of the Grand Cañon.

"Well, fellows," began Ken, "we're started, we're here, and the trip looks great to me. Now, as I am responsible, I intend to be boss. I want you boys to do what I tell you. I may make mistakes, but if I do, I'll take them on my shoulders. Let's try to make the trip a great success. Let's be careful. We're not game-hogs. We'll not kill any more than we can eat. I want you boys to be careful with your guns. Think all the time where you're pointing them. And as to thinking, we'd do well to use our heads all the time. We've no idea what we're going up against in this jungle."

Both boys listened to Ken with attention and respect, but they did not bind themselves by any promises.

Ken had got out the mosquito-netting, expecting any moment to find it very serviceable; however, to his surprise it was not needed. When it came time to go to bed, Hal and George did not forget to slip in between Pepe and Ken. The open-sided tent might keep off rain or dew, but for all the other protection it afforded, the boys might as well have slept outside. Nevertheless they were soon fast asleep. Ken awoke a couple of times during the night and rolled over to find a softer spot in the hard bed. These times he heard only the incessant hum of insects.

When he opened his eyes in the gray morning light, he did hear something that made him sit up with a start.

THE FIRST CAMP

● ● ●

It was a deep booming sound, different from anything that he had ever heard. Ken called Pepe, and that roused the boys.

"Listen," said Ken.

In a little while the sound was repeated, a heavy "boo-oom! . . . boo-oom!" There was a resemblance to the first strong beats of a drumming grouse, only infinitely wilder.

Pepe called it something like *"faisan real."*

"What's that?" asked Hal.

The name was as new to Ken as the noise itself. Pepe explained through George that it was made by a huge black bird not unlike a turkey. It had a golden plume, and could run as fast as a deer. The boys rolled out, all having conceived a desire to see such a strange bird. The sound was not repeated. Almost immediately, however, the thicket across the river awoke to another sound, as much a contrast to the boom as could be imagined. It was a bird medley. At first Ken thought of magpies, but Pepe dispelled this illusion with another name hard to pronounce.

"Chicalocki," he said.

And that seemed just like what they were singing. It was a sharp, clear song—"Chic-a-lock-i . . . chic-a-lock-i," and to judge from the full chorus there must have been many birds.

"They're a kind of pheasant," added George, "and make fine pot-stews."

The *chicalocki* ceased their salute to the morning, and then, as the river mist melted away under the rising sun, other birds took it up. Notes new to Ken burst upon the air. And familiar old songs thrilled him, made

41

him think of summer days on the Susquehanna—the sweet carol of the meadow-lark, the whistle of the quail, the mellow, sad call of the swamp-blackbird. The songs blended in an exquisite harmony.

"Why, some of them are our own birds come south for the winter," declared Hal.

"It's music," said Ken.

"Just wait," laughed George.

It dawned upon Ken then that George was a fellow who had the mysterious airs of a prophet hinting dire things.

Ken did not know what to wait for, but he enjoyed the suggestion and anticipated much. Ducks began to whir by; flocks of blackbirds alighted in the trees across the river. Suddenly Hal jumped up, and Ken was astounded at a great discordant screeching and a sweeping rush of a myriad of wings. Ken looked up to see the largest flock of birds he had ever seen.

"Parrots," he yelled.

Indeed they were, and they let the boys know it. They flew across the river, wheeled to come back, all the time screeching, and then they swept down into the tops of the cypress trees.

"Red-heads," said George. "Just wait till you see the yellow-heads!"

At the moment the red-heads were quite sufficient for Ken. They broke out into a chattering, screaming, cackling discordance. It was plainly directed at the boys. These intelligent birds were curious and resentful. As Pepe put it, they were scolding. Ken enjoyed it for a full half-hour and reveled in the din. That morning serenade was worth the trip. Presently the parrots flew away, and

THE FIRST CAMP

• • •

Ken was surprised to find that most of the other birds had ceased singing. They had set about the business of the day—something it was high time for Ken to consider.

Breakfast over, the boys broke camp, eager for the adventures that they felt to be before them.

6

Wilderness Life

●

"Now for the big job, boys," called Ken. "Any ideas will be welcome, but don't all talk at once."

And this job was the packing of the outfit in the boat. It was a study for Ken, and he found himself thanking his lucky stars that he had packed boats for trips on rapid rivers. George and Hal came to the fore with remarkable advice, which Ken was at the pains of rejecting. And as fast as one wonderful idea emanated from the fertile minds another one came in. At last Ken lost patience.

"Kids, it's going to take brains to pack this boat," he said, with some scorn.

And when Hal remarked that in that case he did not see how they ever were going to pack the boat, Ken drove both boys away and engaged Pepe to help.

The boat had to be packed for a long trip, with many

● ● ●

things taken into consideration. The very best way to
pack it must be decided upon and thereafter held to
strictly. Balance was all-important; comfort and elbow-
room were not to be overlooked; a flat surface easy to
crawl and jump over was absolutely necessary. Fortunately, the boat was large and roomy, although not
heavy. The first thing Ken did was to cut out the narrow
bow-seat. Here, he packed a small bucket of preserved
mullet, some bottles of kerosene and *canya*, and a lan-
tern. The small, flat trunk, full of supplies, went in next.
Two boxes with the rest of the supplies filled up the
space between the trunk and the rowing-seat. By slipping an extra pair of oars, coils of rope, the ax, and a
few other articles between the gunwales and the trunk
and boxes Ken made them fit snugly. He cut off a piece
of the canvas, and, folding it, he laid it with the blankets lengthwise over the top. This made a level surface,
one that could be gotten over quickly, or a place to
sleep, for that matter, and effectually disposed of the
bow half of the boat. Of course the boat sank deep at
the bow, but Ken calculated that when they were all
aboard their weight would effect an even balance.

The bags with clothing Ken put under the second
seat. Then he arranged the other piece of canvas so that
it projected up back of the stern of the boat. He was
thinking of the waves to be buffeted in going stern first
downstream through the rapids. The fishing-tackle and
guns he laid flat from seat to seat. Last of all he placed
the ammunition on one side next the gunwale, and the
suitcase carrying camera, film, and medicines on the
other.

"Come now, fellows," called Ken. "Hal, you and

• • •

George take the second seat. Pepe will take the oars. I'll sit in the stern."

Pepe pushed off, jumped to his place, and grasped the oars. Ken was delighted to find the boat trim, and more buoyant than he had dared to hope.

"We're off," cried Hal, and he whooped. And George exercised his already well-developed faculty of imitating Hal.

Pepe bent to the oars, and under his powerful strokes the boat glided upstream. Soon the bridge disappeared. Ken had expected a long, shady ride, but it did not turn out so. Shallow water and gravelly rapids made rowing impossible.

"Pile out, boys, and pull," said Ken.

The boys had dressed for wading and rough work, and went overboard with a will. Pulling, at first, was not hard work. They were fresh and eager, and hauled the boat up swift, shallow channels, making nearly as good time as when rowing in smooth water. Then, as the sun began to get hot, splashing in the cool river was pleasant. They passed little islands green with willows and came to high clay banks gradually wearing away, and then met with rocky restrictions in the streambed. From round a bend came the hollow roar of a deeper rapid. Ken found it a swiftly rushing incline, very narrow, and hard to pull along. The margin of the river was hidden and obstructed by willows so that the boys could see very little ahead.

When they got above this fall the water was deep and still. Entering the boat again, they turned a curve into a long, beautiful stretch of river.

"Ah! this's something like," said Hal.

WILDERNESS LIFE

• • •

The green, shady lane was alive with birds and water-fowl. Ducks of various kinds rose before the boat. White, blue, gray, and speckled herons, some six feet tall, lined the low bars, and flew only at near approach. There were many varieties of bitterns, one kind with a purple back and white breast. They were very tame and sat on the overhanging branches, uttering dismal croaks. Everywhere was the flash and glitter and gleam of birds in flight, up and down and across the river.

Hal took his camera and tried to get pictures.

The strangeness, beauty, and life of this jungle stream absorbed Ken. He did not take his guns from their cases. The water was bright green and very deep; here and there were the swirls of playing fish. The banks were high and densely covered with a luxuriant foliage. Huge cypress trees, moss-covered, leaned halfway across the river. Giant gray-barked ceibas spread long branches thickly tufted with aloes, orchids, and other jungle parasites. Palm trees lifted slender stems and graceful broad-leaved heads. Clumps of bamboo spread an enormous green arch out over the banks. These bamboo trees were particularly beautiful to Ken. A hundred yellow, black-circled stems grew out of the ground close together, and as they rose high they gracefully leaned their bodies and dropped their tips. The leaves were arrowy, exquisite in their fineness.

He looked up the long river-lane, bright in the sun, dark and still under the moss-veiled cypresses, at the turning vines and blossoming creepers, at the changeful web of moving birds, and indulged to the fullest that haunting sense for wild places.

"Chicalocki," said Pepe, suddenly.

47

KEN WARD IN THE JUNGLE

● ● ●

A flock of long-tailed birds, resembling the pheasant in body, was sailing across the river. Again George made a dive for a gun. This one was a sixteen-gauge and worn out. He shot twice at the birds on the wing. Then Pepe rowed under the overhanging branches, and George killed three *chicalocki* with his rifle. They were olive green in color, and the long tail had a brownish cast. Heavy and plump, they promised fine eating.

"Pato real!" yelled Pepe, pointing excitedly up the river.

Several black fowl, as large as geese, hove in sight, flying pretty low. Ken caught a glimpse of wide, white-crested wings, and knew then that these were the birds he had seen.

"Load up and get ready," he said to George. "They're coming fast—shoot ahead of them."

How swift and powerful they were on the wing! They swooped up when they saw the boat, and offered a splendid target. The little sixteen-gauge rang out. Ken heard the shot strike. The leader stopped in midair, dipped, and plunged with a sounding splash. Ken picked him up and found him to be most beautiful, and as large and heavy as a goose. His black feathers shone with the latent green luster of an opal, and the pure white of the shoulder of the wings made a remarkable contrast.

"George, we've got enough meat for today, more than we can use. Don't shoot any more," said Ken.

Pepe resumed rowing, and Ken told him to keep under the overhanging branches and to row without splashing. He was skilled in the use of the oars, so the boat glided along silently. Ken felt he was rewarded for

● ● ●

this stealth. Birds of rare and brilliant plumage flitted among the branches. There was one, a long, slender bird, gold and black with a white ring round its neck. There were little yellow-breasted kingfishers no larger than a wren, and great red-breasted kingfishers with blue backs and tufted heads. The boat passed under a leaning ceiba tree that was covered with orchids. Ken saw the slim, sharp head of a snake dart from among the leaves. His neck was as thick as Ken's wrist.

"What kind of a snake, Pepe?" whispered Ken, as he fingered the trigger of George's gun. But Pepe did not see the snake, and then Ken thought better of disturbing the silence with a gunshot. He was reminded, however, that the Texan had told him of snakes in this jungle, some of which measured more than fifteen feet and were as large as a man's leg.

Most of the way the bank was too high and steep and overgrown for any animal to get down to the water. Still there were dry gullies, or arroyos, every few hundred yards, and these showed the tracks of animals, but Pepe could not tell what species from the boat. Often Ken heard the pattering of hard feet, and then he would see a little cloud of dust in one of these drinking places. So he cautioned Pepe to row slower and closer in to the bank.

"Look there! Lemme out!" whispered Hal, and he seemed to be on the point of jumping overboard.

"Coons," said George. "Oh, a lot of them. There— some young ones."

Ken saw that they had come abruptly upon a band of racoons, not less than thirty in number, some big, some little, and a few like tiny balls of fur, and all had long

● ● ●

white-ringed tails. What a scampering the big ones set up! The little ones were frightened, and the smallest so tame they scarcely made any effort to escape. Pepe swung the boat in to the bank, and reaching out he caught a baby racoon and handed it to Hal.

"Whoop! We'll catch things and tame them," exclaimed Hal, much delighted, and he proceeded to tie the little racoon under the seat.

"Sure, we'll get a whole menagerie," said George.

So they went on upstream. Often Ken motioned Pepe to stop in dark, cool places under the golden-green canopy of bamboos. He was as much fascinated by the beautiful foliage and tree growths as by the wildlife. Hal appeared more taken up with the fluttering of birds in the thick jungle, rustlings, and soft, stealthy steps. Then as they moved on Ken whispered and pointed out a black animal vanishing in the thicket. Three times he caught sight of a spotted form slipping away in the shade. George saw it the last time, and whispered: "Tiger-cat! Let's get him."

"What's that, Ken, a kind of a wildcat?" asked Hal.

"Yes." Ken took George's .32-caliber and tried to find a way up the bank. There was no place to climb up unless he dragged himself up by the branches of trees or drooping bamboos, and this he did not care to attempt encumbered with a rifle. Only here and there could he see over the matted roots and creepers. Then the sound of rapids put hunting out of his mind.

"Boys, we've got Micas Falls to reach," he said, and told Pepe to row on.

The long stretch of deep river ended in a wide, shallow, noisy rapid. Fir trees lined the banks. The palms, cypresses, bamboos, and the flowery, mossy growths were not here in evidence. Thickly wooded hills rose on each side. The jungle looked sear and yellow.

The boys began to wade up the rapid, and before they had reached the head of it Pepe yelled and jumped back from where he was wading at the bow. He took an oar and began to punch at something in the water, at the same time calling out.

"Crocodile!" cried George, and he climbed in the boat. Hal was not slow in following suit. Then Ken saw Pepe hitting a small crocodile, which lashed out with its tail and disappeared.

"Come out of there," called Ken to the boys. "We can't pull you upstream."

"Say, I don't want to step on one of those ugly brutes," protested Hal.

"Look sharp, then. Come out."

Above the rapid extended a quarter-mile stretch where Pepe could row, and beyond that another long rapid. When the boys had waded up that it was only to come to another. It began to be hard work. But Ken kept the boys buckled down, and they made fair progress. They pulled up through eighteen rapids, and covered distance that Ken estimated to be about ten miles. The blue mountain loomed closer and higher, yet Ken began to have doubts of reaching Micas Falls that day.

Moreover, as they ascended the stream, the rapids grew rougher.

"It'll be great coming down," panted Hal.

Finally they reached a rapid which had long dinned in Ken's ears. All the water in the river rushed down on the right-hand side through a channel scarcely twenty feet wide. It was deep and swift. With the aid of ropes, and by dint of much hard wading and pulling, the boys got the boat up. A little farther on was another bothersome rapid. At last they came to a succession of falls, steps in the river, that barred farther advance upstream.

Here Ken climbed up on the bank, to find the country hilly and open, with patches of jungle and palm groves leading up to the mountains. Then he caught a glint of Micas Falls, and decided that it would be impossible to get there. He made what observations he could, and returned to camp.

"Boys, here's where we stop," said Ken. "It'll be all downstream now, and I'm glad."

There was no doubt that the boys were equally glad. They made camp on a grassy bench above a foam-flecked pool. Ken left the others to get things in shape for supper, and, taking his camera, he hurried off to try to get a picture of Micas Falls. He found open places and by-paths through the brushy forest. He saw evidences of forest fire, and then knew what had ruined that part of the jungle. There were no birds. It was farther than he had estimated to the foothill he had marked, but, loath to give up, he kept on and finally reached a steep, thorny ascent. Going up he nearly suffocated with heat. He felt rewarded for his exertions when he saw Micas Falls glistening in the distance. It was like a string of green fans connected by silver ribbons. He remained there watching it while the sun set in the golden notch between the mountains.

On the way back to camp he waded through a flat overgrown with coarse grass and bushes. Here he

● ● ●

jumped a herd of deer, eight in number. These small, sleek, gray deer appeared tame, and if there had been sufficient light, Ken would have photographed them. It cost him an effort to decide not to fetch his rifle, but as he had meat enough in camp there was nothing to do except let the deer go.

When he got back to the river Pepe grinned at him, and, pointing to little red specks on his shirt, he said:

"Pinilius."

Aha! the ticks!" exclaimed Ken.

They were exceedingly small, not to be seen without close scrutiny. They could not be brushed off, so Ken began laboriously to pick them off. Pepe and George laughed, and Hal appeared to derive some sort of enjoyment from the incident.

"Say, these ticks don't bother me any," declared Ken.

Pepe grunted, and George called out, "Just wait till you get the big fellows—the garrapatoes."

It developed presently that the grass and bushes on the camp-site contained millions of the ticks. Ken found several of the larger ticks—almost the size of his little fingernail—but he did not get bitten. Pepe and George, however, had no such good luck, as was manifested at different times. By the time they had cut down the bushes and carried in a stock of firewood, both were covered with the little pests. Hal found a spot where there appeared to be none, and here he stayed.

Pepe and George had the bad habit of smoking, and Ken saw them burning the ticks off shirt-sleeves and trouser-legs, using the fiery ends of their cigarettes. This feat did not puzzle Ken anything like the one where they held the red points of the cigarettes close to their naked flesh. Ken, and Hal, too, had to see that performance at close range.

"Why do you do that?" asked Ken.

"Popping ticks," replied George. He and Pepe were as sober as judges.

The fact of the matter was soon clear to Ken. The ticks stuck on as if glued. When the hot end of the burning cigarette was held within a quarter of an inch of them they simply blew up, exploded with a pop. Ken could easily distinguish between the tiny pop of an exploding *pinilius* and the heavier pop of a *garrapato*.

"But, boy, while you're taking time to do that, half a dozen other ticks can bite you!" exclaimed Ken.

"Sure they can," replied George. "But if they get on me I'll kill 'em. I don't mind the little ones—it's the big boys I hate."

On the other hand, Pepe seemed to mind most the *pinilius*.

"Say, from now on you fellows will be Garrapato George and Pinilius Pepe."

"Pretty soon you'll laugh on the other side of your face," said George. "In three days you'll be popping ticks yourself."

Just then Hal let out a yell and began to hunt for a tick that had bit him. If there was anything that could bother Hal Ward it was a crawling bug of some kind.

"I'll have to christen you, too, brother," said Ken, gurgling with mirth. "A very felicitous name— Hollering Hal!"

Despite the humor of the thing, Ken really saw its serious side. When he found the grass under his feet alive

● ● ●

with ticks he cast about in his mind for some way to get rid of them. And he hit upon a remedy. On the ridge above the bench was a palm tree, and under it were many dead palm leaves. These were large in size, had long stems, and were as dry as tinder. Ken lighted one, and it made a flaming hot torch. It did not take him long to scorch all the ticks near that camp.

The boys had supper and enjoyed it hugely. The scene went well with the camp-fire and game dinner. They gazed out over the foaming pool, the brawling rapids, to the tufted palm trees, and above them the dark blue mountain. At dusk, Hal and George were so tired they went to bed and at once dropped into slumber. Pepe sat smoking before the slumbering fire.

And Ken chose that quiet hour to begin the map of the river, and to set down in his notebook his observations on the mountains and in the valley, and what he had seen that day of bird, animal, and plant life in the jungle.

7

Running the Rapids

●

Some time in the night a yell awakened Ken. He sat up, clutching his revolver. The white moonlight made all as clear as day. Hal lay deep in slumber. George was raising himself, half aroused. But Pepe was gone.

Ken heard a thrashing about outside. Leaping up he ran out, and was frightened to see Pepe beating and clawing and tearing at himself like a man possessed of demons.

"Pepe, what's wrong?" shouted Ken.

It seemed that Pepe only grew more violent in his wrestling about. Then Ken was sure Pepe had been stung by a scorpion or bitten by a snake.

But he was dumbfounded to see George bound like an apparition out of the tent and begin evolutions that made Pepe's look slow.

RUNNING THE RAPIDS

● ● ●

"Hey, what's wrong with you jumping-jacks?" yelled Ken.

George was as grimly silent as an Indian running the gauntlet, but Ken thought it doubtful if any Indian ever slapped and tore at his body in George's frantic manner. To add to the mystery Hal suddenly popped out of the tent. He was yelling in a way to do justice to the name Ken had lately given him, and, as for wild and whirling antics, his were simply marvelous.

"Good land!" ejaculated Ken. Had the boys all gone mad? Despite his alarm, Ken had to roar with laughter at those three dancing figures in the moonlight. A rush of ideas went through Ken's confused mind. And the last prompted him to look in the tent.

He saw a wide bar of black crossing the moonlit ground, the grass, and the blankets. This bar moved. It was alive. Bending low Ken descried that it was made by ants. An army of jungle ants on a march! They had come in a straight line along the base of the little hill, and their passageway led under the canvas. Pepe happened to be the first in line, and they had surged over him. As he had awakened, and jumped up of course, the ants had begun to bite. The same in turn had happened to George and then Hal.

Ken was immensely relieved, and had his laugh out. The stream of ants moved steadily and quite rapidly, and soon passed from sight. By this time Pepe and the boys had threshed themselves free of ants and into some degree of composure.

"Say, you nightmare fellows! Come back to bed," said Ken. "Anyone would think something had really happened to you."

● ● ●

Pepe snorted, which made Ken think the native understood something of English. And the boys grumbled loudly.

"Ants! Ants as big as wasps! They bit worse than helgramites," declared Hal. "Oh, they missed you. You always are lucky. I'm not afraid of all the old jaguars in this jungle. But I can't stand biting, crawling bugs. I wish you hadn't made me come on this darn trip."

"Ha! Ha!" laughed Ken.

"Just wait, Hal," put in George, grimly. "Just wait. It's coming to him!"

The boys slept well the remainder of the night and, owing to the break in their rest, did not awaken early. The sun shone hot when Ken rolled out; a creamy mist was dissolving over the curve of the mountain range; parrots were screeching in the nearby trees.

After breakfast Ken set about packing the boat as it had been done the day before.

"I think we'll do well to leave the trunk in the boat after this, unless we find a place where we want to make a permanent camp for a while," said Ken.

Before departing he carefully looked over the ground to see that nothing was left, and espied a heavy fish-line which George had baited, set, and forgotten.

"Hey, George, pull up your trot-line. It looks pretty much stretched to me. Maybe you've got a fish."

Ken happened to be busy at the boat when George started to take in the line. An exclamation from Pepe,

RUNNING THE RAPIDS

● ● ●

George's yell, and a loud splash made Ken jump up in double-quick time. Hal also came running.

George was staggering on the bank, leaning back hard on the heavy line. A long, angry swirl in the pool told of a powerful fish. It was likely to pull George in.

"Let go the line!" yelled Ken.

But George was not letting go of any fish-lines. He yelled for Pepe, and went down on his knees before Pepe got to him. Both then pulled on the line. The fish, or whatever it was at the other end, gave a mighty jerk that almost dragged the two off the bank.

"Play him, play him!" shouted Ken. "You've got plenty of line. Give him some."

Hal now added his weight and strength, and the three of them, unmindful of Ken's advice, hauled back with might and main. The line parted and they sprawled on the grass.

"What a sockdologer!" exclaimed Hal.

"I had that hook baited with a big piece of duck meat," said George. "We must have been hooked to a crocodile. Things are happening to us."

"Yes, so I've noticed," replied Ken, dryly. "But if you fellows hadn't pulled so hard you might have landed that thing, whatever it was. All aboard now. We must be on the move—we don't know what we have before us."

When they got into the boat Ken took the oars, much to Pepe's surprise. It was necessary to explain to him that Ken would handle the boat in swift water. They shoved off, and Ken sent one regretful glance up the

river, at the shady aisle between the green banks, at the
white rapids, and at the great colored dome of the
mountain. He almost hesitated, for he desired to see
more of that jungle-covered mountain. But something
already warned Ken to lose no time in the trip down the
Santa Rosa. There did not seem to be any reason for
hurry, yet he felt it necessary. But he asked Pepe many
questions and kept George busy interpreting names of
trees and flowers and wild creatures.

Going downstream on any river, mostly, would have
been pleasurable, but drifting on the swift current of the
Santa Rosa and rowing under the wonderful moss-
bearded cypresses was almost like a dream. It was too
beautiful to seem real. The smooth stretch before the
first rapid was short, however, and then all Ken's attention had to be given to the handling of the boat. He saw
that George and Pepe both expected to get out and wade
down the rapids as they had waded up. He had a surprise in store for them. The rapids that he could not
shoot would have to be pretty bad.

"You're getting close," shouted George, warningly.

With two sweeps of the oars Ken turned the boat
stern first downstream, then dipped on the low green incline, and sailed down toward the waves. They struck
the first wave with a shock, and the water flew all over
the boys. Pepe was tremendously excited; he yelled and
made wild motions with his hands; George looked a little frightened. Hal enjoyed it. Whatever the rapid appeared to them, it was magnificent to Ken; and it was
play to manage the boat in such water. A little pull on
one oar and then on the other kept the stern straight

RUNNING THE RAPIDS

• • •

downstream. The channel he could make out a long way ahead. He amused himself by watching George and Pepe. There were stones in the channel, and the water rose angrily about them. A glance was enough to tell that he could float over these without striking. But the boys thought they were going to hit every stone, and were uneasy all the time. Twice he had to work to pass ledges and sunken trees upon which the current bore down hard. When Ken neared one of these he dipped the oars and pulled back to stop or lessen the momentum; then a stroke turned the boat half broadside to the current. That would force it to one side, and another stroke would turn the boat straight. At the bottom of this rapid they encountered a long triangle of choppy waves that they bumped and splashed over. They came through with nothing wet but the raised flap of canvas in the stern.

Pepe regarded Ken with admiring eyes, and called him *grande mozo*.

"Shooting rapids is great sport," proclaimed George.

They drifted through several little rifts, and then stopped at the head of the narrow chute that had been such a stumbling block on the way up. Looked at from above, this long, narrow channel, with several S curves, was a fascinating bit of water for a canoeist. It tempted Ken to shoot it even with the boat. But he remembered the four-foot waves at the bottom, and besides he resented the importunity of the spirit of daring so early in the game. Risk, and perhaps peril, would come soon enough. So he decided to walk along the shore and float the boat through with a rope.

• • •

The thing looked a good deal easier than it turned out to be. Halfway through, at the narrowest point and most abrupt curve, Pepe misunderstood directions and pulled hard on the bow-rope, when he should have let it slack.

The boat swung in, nearly smashing Ken against the bank, and the sweeping current began to swell dangerously near the gunwale.

"Let go! Let go!" yelled Ken. "George, make him let go!"

But George, who was trying to get the rope out of Pepe's muscular hands, suddenly made a dive for his rifle.

"Deer! deer!" he cried, hurriedly throwing a shell into the chamber. He shot downstream, and Ken, looking that way, saw several deer under the firs on a rocky flat. George shot three more times, and the bullets went "spinging" into the trees. The deer bounded out of sight.

When Ken turned again, water was roaring into the boat. He was being pressed harder into the bank, and he saw disaster ahead.

"Loosen the rope—tell him, George," yelled Ken.

Pepe only pulled the harder.

"Quick, or we're ruined," cried Ken.

George shouted in Spanish, and Pepe promptly dropped the rope in the water. That was the worst thing he could have done.

"Grab the rope!" ordered Ken, wildly. "Grab the bow! Don't let it swing out! Hal!"

Before either boy could reach it the bow swung out

• • •

into the current. Ken was not only helpless, but in a dangerous position. He struggled to get out from where the swinging stern was wedging him into the bank, but could not budge. Fearing that all the outfit would be lost in the river, he held on to the boat and called for someone to catch the rope.

George pushed Pepe head first into the swift current. Pepe came up, caught the rope, and then went under again. The boat swung round and, now half full of water, got away from Ken. It gathered headway. Ken leaped out on the ledge and ran along with the boat. It careened round the bad curve and shot downstream. Pepe was still under water.

"He's drowned! He's drowned!" cried George.

Hal took a header right off the ledge, came up, and swam with a few sharp strokes to the drifting boat. He gained the bow, grasped it, and then pulled on the rope.

Ken had a sickening feeling that Pepe might be drowned. Suddenly Pepe appeared like a brown porpoise. He was touching bottom in places and holding back on the rope. Then the current rolled him over and over. The boat drifted back of a rocky point into shallow water. Hal gave a haul that helped to swing it out of the dangerous current. Then Pepe came up, and he, too, pulled hard. Just as Ken plunged in the boat sank in two feet of water. Ken's grip, containing camera, film, and other perishable goods, was on top, and he got it just in time. He threw it out on the rocks. Then together the boys lifted the boat and hauled the bow well up on the shore.

● ● ●

"Pretty lucky!" exclaimed Ken, as he flopped down.

"Doggone it!" yelled Hal, suddenly. And he dove for the boat, and splashed round in the water under his seat to bring forth a very limp and drenched little raccoon.

"Good! He's all right," said Ken.

Pepe said, "Mucho malo," and pointed to his shins, which bore several large bumps from contact with the rocks in the channel.

"I should say mucha malo," growled George.

He jerked open his grip, and, throwing out articles of wet clothing—for which he had no concern—he gazed in dismay at his whole store of cigarettes wet by the water.

"So that's all you care for," said Ken, severely. "Young man, I'll have something to say to you presently. All hands now to unpack the boat."

Fortunately nothing had been carried away. That part of the supplies which would have been affected by water was packed in tin cases, and so suffered no damage. The ammunition was waterproof. Ken's Parker hammerless and his .351 automatic rifle were full of water, and so were George's guns and Hal's. While they took their weapons apart, wiped them, and laid them in the sun, Pepe spread out the rest of the things and then baled out the boat. The sun was so hot that everything dried quickly and was not any the worse for the wetting. The boys lost scarcely an hour by the accident. Before the start Ken took George and Pepe to task, and when he finished they were both very sober and quiet.

RUNNING THE RAPIDS

● ● ●

Ken observed, however, that by the time they had run the next rapid they were enjoying themselves again. Then came a long succession of rapids which Ken shot without anything approaching a mishap. When they drifted into the level stretch Pepe relieved him at the oars. They glided downstream under the drooping bamboo, under the silken streamers of silvery moss, under the dark, cool bowers of matted vine and blossoming creepers. And as they passed this time the jungle silence awoke to the crack of George's .22 and the discordant cry of river fowl. Ken's guns were both at hand, and the rifle was loaded, but he did not use either. He contented himself with snapping a picture here and there and watching the bamboo thickets and the mouths of the little dry ravines.

That ride was again so interesting, so full of sound and action and color, that it seemed a very short one. The murmur of the water on the rocks told Ken that it was time to change seats with Pepe. They drifted down two short rapids, and then came to the gravelly channels between the islands noted on the way up. The water was shallow down these rippling channels; and, fearing they might strike a stone, Ken tumbled out over the bow and, wading slowly, let the boat down to still water again. He was about to get in when he espied what he thought was an alligator lying along a log near the river. He pointed it out to Pepe.

That worthy yelled gleefully in Mexican, and reached for his *machete*.

"Iguana!" exclaimed George. "I've heard it's good to eat."

65

KEN WARD IN THE JUNGLE

• • •

The reptile had a body about four feet long and a very long tail. Its color was a steely blue-black on top, and it had a blunt, rounded head.

Pepe slipped out of the boat and began to wade ashore. When the iguana raised itself on short, stumpy legs George shot at it, and missed, as usual. But he effectually frightened the reptile, which started to climb the bank with much nimbleness. Pepe began to run, brandishing his long *machete*. George plunged into the water in hot pursuit, and then Hal yielded to the call of the chase. Pepe reached the iguana before it got up the bank, aimed a mighty blow with his *machete*, and would surely have cut the reptile in two pieces if the blade had not caught on an overhanging branch. Then Pepe fell up the bank and barely grasped the tail of the iguana. Pepe hauled back, and Pepe was powerful. The frantic creature dug its feet in the clay bank and held on for dear life. But Pepe was too strong. He jerked the iguana down and flung it square upon George, who had begun to climb the bank.

George uttered an awful yell, as if he expected to be torn asunder, and rolled down, with the reptile on top of him. Ken saw that it was as badly frightened as George. But Hal did not see this. And he happened to have gained a little sand-bar below the bank, in which direction the iguana started with wonderful celerity. Then Hal made a jump that Ken believed was a record.

Remarkably awkward as that iguana was, he could surely cover ground with his stumpy legs. Again he dashed up the bank. Pepe got close enough once more,

● ● ●

and again he swung the *machete*. The blow cut off a piece of the long tail, but the only effect this produced was to make the iguana run all the faster. It disappeared over the bank, with Pepe scrambling close behind. Then followed a tremendous crashing in the dry thickets, after which the iguana could be heard rattling and tearing away through the jungle. Pepe returned to the boat with the crestfallen boys, and he was much concerned over the failure to catch the big lizard, which he said made fine eating.

"What next?" asked George, ruefully, and at that the boys all laughed.

"The fun is we don't have any idea what's coming off," said Hal.

"Boys, if you brave hunters had thought to throw a little salt on that lizard's tail you might have caught him," added Ken.

Presently Pepe espied another iguana in the forks of a tree, and he rowed ashore. This lizard was only a small one, not over two feet in length, but he created some excitement among the boys. George wanted him to eat, and Hal wanted the skin for a specimen, and Ken wanted to see what the lizard looked like close at hand. So they all clamored for Pepe to use caution and to be quick.

When Pepe started up the tree the iguana came down on the other side, quick as a squirrel. Then they had a race round the trunk until Pepe ended it with a well-directed blow from his *machete*.

Hal began to skin the iguana.

"Ken, I'm going to have trouble preserving specimens in this hot place," he said.

● ● ●

"Salt and alum will do the trick. Remember what old Hiram used to say," replied Ken.

Shortly after that the boat passed the scene of the first camp, and then drifted under the railroad bridge.

Hal and George, and Pepe, too, looked as if they were occupied with the same thought troubling Ken— that once beyond the bridge they would plunge into the jungle wilderness from which there could be no turning back.

8

The First Tiger-cat

•

The Santa Rosa opened out wide, and ran swiftly over smooth rock. Deep cracks, a foot or so wide, crossed the river diagonally, and fish darted in and out.

The boys had about half a mile of this, when, after turning a hilly bend, they entered a long rapid. It was a wonderful stretch of river to look down.

"By George!" said Ken, as he stood up to survey it. "This is great!"

"It's all right *now*," added George, with his peculiar implication as to the future.

"What gets me is the feeling of what might be round the next bend," said Hal.

This indeed, Ken thought, made the fascination of such travel. The water was swift and smooth and shallow. There was scarcely a wave or ripple. At times the boat stuck fast on the flat rock, and the boys would

• • •

have to get out to shove off. As far ahead as Ken could see extended this wide slant of water. On the left rose a thick line of huge cypresses all festooned with gray moss that drooped to the water; on the right rose a bare bluff of crumbling rock. It looked like blue clay baked and cracked by the sun. A few palms fringed the top.

"Say, we can beat this," said Ken, as for the twentieth time the boys had to step out and shove off a flat, shallow place. "Two of you in the bow and Pepe with me in the stern, feet overboard."

The little channels ran every way, making it necessary to turn the boat often. Ken's idea was to drift along and keep the boat from grounding by an occasional kick.

"Ken manages to think of something once in a while," observed Hal.

Then the boat drifted downstream, whirling round and round. Here Pepe would drop his brown foot in and kick his end clear of a shallow ledge; there George would make a great splash when his turn came to ward off from a rock; and again Hal would give a greater kick than was necessary to the righting of the boat. Probably Hal was much influenced by the fact that when he kicked hard he destroyed the lazy equilibrium of his companions.

It dawned upon Ken that here was a new and unique way to travel down a river. It was different from anything he had ever tried before. The water was swift and seldom more than a foot deep, except in diagonal cracks that ribbed the riverbed. This long, shut-in stretch appeared to be endless. But for the quick, gliding movement of the boat, which made a little breeze, the heat would have been intolerable. When one of Hal's kicks made Ken lurch overboard to sit down ludicrously, the cool water sent thrills over him. Instead of retaliating on Hal, he was glad to be wet. And the others, soon discovering the reason for Ken's remarkable good nature, went overboard and lay flat in the cool ripples. Then little clouds of steam began to rise from their soaked clothes.

Ken began to have an idea that he had been wise in boiling the water which they drank. They all suffered from a parching thirst. Pepe scooped up water in his hand; George did likewise, and then Hal.

"You've all got to stop that," ordered Ken, sharply. "No drinking this water unless it's boiled."

The boys obeyed, for the hour, but they soon forgot, or deliberately allayed their thirst despite Ken's command. Ken himself found his thirst unbearable. He squeezed the juice of a wild lime into a cup of water and drank that. Then he insisted on giving the boys doses of quinine and anti-malaria pills, which treatment he meant to continue daily.

Toward the lower part of that rapid, where the water grew deeper, fish began to be so numerous that the boys kicked at many as they darted under the boat. There were thousands of small fish and some large ones. Occasionally, as a big fellow lunged for a crack in the rock, he would make the water roar. There was a fish that resembled a mullet, and another that Hal said was some kind of bass with a blue tail. Pepe chopped at them with his *machete*; George whacked with an oar; Hal stood up in the boat and shot at them with his .22 rifle.

KEN WARD IN THE JUNGLE

● ● ●

"Say, I've got to see what that blue-tailed bass looks like," said Ken. "You fellows will never get one."

Whereupon Ken jointed up a small rod and, putting on a spinner, began to cast it about. He felt two light fish hit it. Then came a heavy shock that momentarily checked the boat. The water foamed as the line cut through, and Ken was just about to jump off the boat to wade and follow the fish, when it broke the leader.

"That was a fine exhibition," remarked the critical Hal.

"What's the matter with you?" retorted Ken, who was sensitive as to his fishing abilities. "It was a big fish. He broke things."

"Haven't you got a reel on that rod and fifty yards of line?" queried Hal.

Ken did not have another spinner, and he tried an artificial minnow, but could not get a strike on it. He took Hal's gun and shot at several of the blue-tailed fish, but though he made them jump out of the water like a real northern black bass, it was all of no avail.

Then Hal caught one with a swoop of the landing net. It was a beautiful fish, and it did have a blue tail. Pepe could not name it, nor could Ken classify it, so Hal was sure he had secured a rare specimen.

When the boat drifted round a bend to enter another long, wide, shallow rapid, the boys demurred a little at the sameness of things. The bare blue bluffs persisted, and the line of gray-veiled cypresses and the strange formation of stream bed. Five more miles of drifting under the glaring sun made George and Hal lie back in the boat, under an improvised sun-shade. The ride was novel and strange to Ken Ward, and did not pall upon

THE FIRST TIGER-CAT

● ● ●

him, though he suffered from the heat and glare. He sat on the bow, occasionally kicking the boat off a rock.

All at once a tense whisper from Pepe brought Ken round with a jerk. Pepe was pointing down along the right-hand shore. George heard, and, raising himself, called excitedly: "Buck! Buck!"

Ken saw a fine deer leap back from the water and start to climb the side of a gully that indented the bluff. Snatching up the .351 rifle, he shoved in the safety catch. The distance was far—perhaps two hundred yards—but without elevating the sights he let drive. A cloud of dust puffed up under the nose of the climbing deer.

"Wow!" yelled George, and Pepe began to jabber. Hal sprang up, nearly falling overboard, and he shouted: "Give it to him, Ken!"

The deer bounded up a steep, winding trail, his white flag standing, his reddish coat glistening. Ken fired again. The bullet sent up a white puff of dust, this time nearer still. That shot gave Ken the range, and he pulled the automatic again—and again. Each bullet hit closer. The boys were now holding their breath, watching, waiting. Ken aimed a little firmer and finer at the space ahead of the deer—for in that instant he remembered what the old hunter on Penetier had told him—and he pulled the trigger twice.

The buck plunged down, slipped off the trail, and, raising a cloud of dust, rolled over and over. Then it fell sheer into space, and whirled down to strike the rock with a sodden crash.

It was Ken's first shooting on this trip, and he could

● ● ●

not help adding a cry of exultation to the yells of his admiring comrades.

"Guess you didn't plug him!" exclaimed Hal Ward, with flashing eyes.

Wading, the boys pulled the boat ashore. Pepe pronounced the buck to be very large, but to Ken, remembering the deer in Coconino Forest, it appeared small. If there was an unbroken bone left in that deer, Ken greatly missed his guess. He and Pepe cut out the haunch least crushed by the fall.

"There's no need to carry along more meat than we can use," said George. "It spoils overnight. That's the worst of this jungle, I've heard hunters say."

Hal screwed up his face in the manner he affected when he tried to imitate old Hiram Bent. "Wal, youngster, I reckon I'm right an' down proud of thet shootin'. You air comin' along."

Ken was as pleased as Hal, but he replied, soberly: "Well, kid, I hope I can hold as straight as that when we run up against a jaguar."

"Do you think we'll see one?" asked Hal.

"Just you wait!" exclaimed George, replying for Ken. "Pepe says we'll have to sleep in the boat, and anchor the boat in the middle of the river."

"What for?"

"To keep those big yellow tigers from eating us up."

"How nice!" replied Hal, with a rather forced laugh.

So, talking and laughing, the boys resumed their downstream journey. Ken, who was always watching with sharp eyes, saw buzzards appear, as if by magic. Before the boat was half a mile down the river buzzards were circling over the remains of the deer. These birds of prey did not fly from the jungle on either side of the stream. They sailed, then dropped down from the clear blue sky where they had been invisible. How wonderful that was to Ken! Nature had endowed these vulture-like birds with wonderful scent or instinct or sight, or all combined. But Ken believed that it was power of sight which brought the buzzards so quickly to the scene of the killing. He watched them circling, sweeping down till a curve in the river hid them from view.

And with this bend came a welcome change. The bluff played out in a rocky slope below which the green jungle was relief to aching eyes. As the boys made this point, the evening breeze began to blow. They beached the boat and unloaded to make camp.

"We haven't had any work today, but we're all tired just the same," observed Ken.

"The heat makes a fellow tired," said George.

They were fortunate in finding a grassy plot where there appeared to be but few ticks and other creeping things. That evening it was a little surprise to Ken to realize how sensitive he had begun to feel about these jungle vermin.

Pepe went up the bank for firewood. Ken heard him slashing away with his *machete*. Then this sound ceased, and Pepe yelled in fright. Ken and George caught up guns as they bounded into the thicket; Hal started to follow, likewise armed. Ken led the way through a thorny brake to come suddenly upon Pepe. At the same instant Ken caught a glimpse of gray, black-striped forms slipping away in the jungle. Pepe shouted out something.

"Tiger-cats!" exclaimed George.

KEN WARD IN THE JUNGLE

• • •

Ken held up his finger to enjoin silence. With that he stole cautiously forward, the others noiselessly at his heels. The thicket was lined with well-beaten trails, and by following these and stooping low it was possible to go ahead without rustling the brush. Owing to the gathering twilight Ken could not see very far. When he stopped to listen he heard the faint crackling of dead brush and soft, quick steps. He had not proceeded far when pattering footsteps halted him. Ken dropped to his knee. The boys knelt behind him, and Pepe whispered. Peering along the trail Ken saw what he took for a wildcat. Its boldness amazed him. Surely it had heard him, but instead of bounding into the thicket it crouched not more than twenty-five feet away. Ken took a quick shot at the gray huddled form. It jerked, stretched out, and lay still. Then a crashing in the brush, and gray streaks down the trail told Ken of more game.

"There they go. Peg away at them," called Ken.

George and Hal burned a good deal of powder and sent much lead whistling through the dry branches, but the gray forms vanished in the jungle.

"We got one, anyway," said Ken.

He advanced to find his quarry quite dead. It was bigger than any wildcat Ken had ever seen. The color was a grayish yellow, almost white, lined and spotted with black. Ken lifted it and found it heavy enough to make a good load.

"He's a beauty," said Hal.

"Pepe says it's a tiger-cat," remarked George. "There are two or three kinds besides the big tiger. We may run into a lot of them and get some skins."

It was almost dark when they reached camp. While

76

THE FIRST TIGER-CAT

● ● ●

Pepe and Hal skinned the tiger-cat and stretched the pelt over a framework of sticks the other boys got supper. They were all very hungry and tired, and pleased with the events of the day. As they sat round the campfire there was a constant whirring of water-fowl over their heads and an incessant hum of insects from the jungle.

"Ken, does it feel as wild to you here as on Buckskin Mountain?" asked Hal.

"Oh yes, much wilder, Hal," replied his brother. "And it's different, somehow. Out in Arizona there was always the glorious expectancy of tomorrow's fun or sport. Here I have a kind of worry—a feeling—"

But he concluded it wiser to keep to himself that strange feeling of dread which came over him at odd moments.

"It suits me," said Hal. "I want to get a lot of things and keep them alive. Of course, I want specimens. I'd like some skins for my den, too. But I don't care so much about killing things."

"Just wait!" retorted George, who evidently took Hal's remark as a reflection upon his weakness. "Just wait! You'll be shooting pretty soon for your life."

"Now, George, what do you mean by that?" questioned Ken, determined to pin George down to facts. "You said you didn't really *know* anything about this jungle. Why are you always predicting disaster for us?"

"Why? Because I've heard things about the jungle," retorted George. "And Pepe says wait till we get down off the mountain. He doesn't *know* anything, either. But it's his instinct—Pepe's half Indian. So I say, too, wait till we get down in the jungle!"

• • •

"Confound you! Where are we now?" queried Ken.

"The real jungle is the lowland. There we'll find the tigers and the crocodiles and the wild cattle and wild pigs."

"Bring on your old pigs and things," replied Hal.

But Ken looked into the glowing embers of the camp-fire and was silent. When he got out his note-book and began his drawing, he forgot the worry and dread in the interest of his task. He was astonished at his memory, to see how he could remember every turn in the river and yet not lose his sense of direction. He could tell almost perfectly the distance traveled, because he knew so well just how much a boat would cover in swift or slow waters in a given time. He thought he could give a fairly correct estimate of the drop of the river. And, as for descriptions of the jungle life along the shores, that was a delight, all except trying to under-stand and remember and spell the names given to him by Pepe. Ken imagined Pepe spoke a mixture of Toltec, Aztec, Indian, Spanish, and English.

9

In the White Water

●

Upon awakening next morning Ken found the sun an hour high. He was stiff and sore and thirsty. Pepe and the boys slept so soundly it seemed selfish to wake them.

All around camp there was a melodious concourse of birds. But the parrots did not make a visit that morning. While Ken was washing in the river a troop of deer came down to the bar on the opposite side. Ken ran for his rifle, and by mistake took up George's .32. He had a splendid shot at less than one hundred yards. But the bullet dropped fifteen feet in front of the leading buck. The deer ran into the deep, bushy willows.

"That gun's leaded," muttered Ken. "It didn't shoot where I aimed."

Pepe jumped up; George rolled out of his blanket with one eye still glued shut; and Hal stretched and yawned and groaned.

KEN WARD IN THE JUNGLE

• • •

"Do I *have* to get up?" he asked.

"Shore, lad," said Ken, mimicking Jim Williams, "or I'll hev to be reconsiderin' that idee of mine about you bein' pards with me."

Such mention of Hal's ranger friend brought the boy out of his lazy bed with amusing alacrity.

"Rustle breakfast, now, you fellows," said Ken, and, taking his rifle, he started off to climb the high river bluff.

It was his idea to establish firmly in mind the trend of the mountain range and the relation of the river to it. The difficulty in mapping the river would come after it left the mountains to wind away into the wide lowlands. The matter of climbing the bluff would have been easy but for the fact that he wished to avoid contact with grass, brush, trees, even dead branches, as all were covered with ticks. The upper half of the bluff was bare, and when he reached that part he soon surmounted it. Ken faced south with something of eagerness. Fortunately the mist had dissolved under the warm rays of the sun, affording an unobstructed view. That scene was wild and haunting, yet different from what his fancy had pictured. The great expanse of jungle was gray, the green line of cypress, palm, and bamboo following the southward course of the river. The mountain range some ten miles distant sloped to the south and faded away in the haze. The river disappeared in rich dark verdure, and but for it, which afforded a water-road back to civilization, Ken would have been lost in a dense gray-green overgrowth of tropical wilderness. Once or twice he thought he caught the faint roar of a waterfall on the morning breeze, yet could not be sure, and he turned toward camp with a sober appreciation of the difficulty of his enterprise and a more thrilling sense of its hazard and charm.

"Didn't see anything *to* peg at, eh?" greeted Hal. "Well, get your teeth in some of this venison before it's all gone."

Soon they were under way again, Pepe strong and willing at the oars. This time Ken had his rifle and shot-gun close at hand, ready for use. Half a mile below, the river, running still and deep, entered a shaded waterway so narrow that in places the branches of wide-spreading and leaning cypresses met and intertwined their moss-fringed foliage. This lane was a paradise for birds that ranged from huge speckled cranes, six feet high, to little yellow birds almost too small to see.

Black squirrels were numerous and very tame. In fact, all the creatures along this shaded stream were so fearless that it was easy to see they had never heard a shot. Ken awoke sleepy cranes with his fishing-rod and once pushed a blue heron off a log. He heard animals of some species running back from the bank, but could not see them.

All at once a soft breeze coming upstream bore the deep roar of tumbling rapids. The sensation of dread which had bothered Ken occasionally now returned and fixed itself in his mind. He was in the jungle of Mexico, and knew not what lay ahead of him. But if he had been in the wilds of unexplored Brazil and had heard that roar, it would have been familiar to him. In his canoe experience on the swift streams of Pennsylvania Ken

KEN WARD IN THE JUNGLE

● ● ●

Ward had learned, long before he came to rapids, to judge what they were from the sound. His attention wandered from the beautiful birds, the moss-shaded bowers, and the overhanging jungle. He listened to the heavy, sullen roar of the rapids.

"That water sounds different," remarked George.

"Grande," said Pepe, with a smile.

"Pretty heavy, Ken, eh?" asked Hal, looking quickly at his brother.

But Ken Ward made his face a mask, and betrayed nothing of the grim nature of his thought. Pepe and the boys had little idea of danger, and they had now a blind faith in Ken.

"I dare say we'll get used to that roar," replied Ken, easily, and he began to pack his guns away in their cases.

Hal forgot his momentary anxiety; Pepe rowed on, leisurely; and George lounged in his seat. There was no menace for them in that dull, continuous roar.

But Ken knew they would soon be in fast water and before long would drop down into the real wilderness. It was not now too late to go back up the river, but soon that would be impossible. Keeping a sharp lookout ahead, Ken revolved in mind the necessity for caution and skilful handling of the boat. But he realized, too, that overzealousness on the side of caution was a worse thing for such a trip than sheer recklessness. Good judgment in looking over rapids, a quick eye to pick the best channel, then a daring spirit—that was the ideal to be striven for in going down swift rivers.

Presently Ken saw a break in the level surface of the water. He took Pepe's place at the oars, and, as usual, turned the boat stern first downstream. The banks were low and shelved out in rocky points. This relieved Ken, for he saw that he could land just above the falls. What he feared was a narrow gorge impossible to portage round or go through. As the boat approached the break the roar seemed to divide itself, hollow and shallow near at hand, rushing and heavy farther on.

Ken rowed close to the bank and landed on the first strip of rock. He got out and, walking along this ledge, soon reached the fall. It was a straight drop of some twelve or fifteen feet. The water was shallow all the way across.

"Boys, this is easy," said Ken. "We'll pack the outfit round the fall, and slide the boat over."

But Ken did not say anything about the white water extending below the fall as far as he could see. From here came the sullen roar that had worried him.

Portaging the supplies around that place turned out to be far from easy. The portage was not long nor rugged, but the cracked, water-worn rock made going very difficult. The boys often stumbled. Pepe fell and broke open a box, and almost broke his leg. Ken had a hard knock. Then, when it came to carrying the trunk, one at each corner, progress was laborious and annoying. Full two hours were lost in transporting the outfit around the fall.

Below there was a wide, shelving apron, over which the water ran a foot or so in depth. Ken stationed Pepe and the boys there, and went up to get the boat. He waded out with it. Ken saw that his end of this business was going to be simple enough, but he had doubts as to what would happen to the boys.

"Brace yourselves, now," he yelled. "When I drop her over she'll come a-humming. Hang on if she drags you a mile!"

Wading out deeper Ken let the boat swing down with the current till the stern projected over the fall. He had trouble in keeping his footing, for the rock was slippery. Then with a yell he ran the stern far out over the drop, bore down hard on the bow, and shoved off.

The boat shot out and down, to alight with a heavy souse. Then it leaped into the swift current. George got his hands on it first, and went down like a ninepin. The boat floated over him. The bow struck Hal, and would have dragged him away had not Pepe laid powerful hands on the stern. They waded to the lower ledge.

"Didn't ship a bucketful," said Hal. "Fine work, Ken."

"I got all the water," added the drenched and dripping George.

"Bail out, boys, and repack, while I look below," said Ken.

He went downstream a little way to take a survey of the rapids. If those rapids had been back in Pennsylvania, Ken felt that he could have gone at them in delight. If the jungle country had been such that damage to boat or supplies could have been remedied or replaced, these rapids would not have appeared so bad. Ken walked up and down looking over the long white inclines more than was wise, and he hesitated about going into them. But it had to be done. So he went back to the boys. Then he took the oars with gripping fingers.

"George, can you swim?" he asked.

"I'm a second cousin to a fish," replied George.

IN THE WHITE WATER

● ● ●

"All right. We're off. Now, if we upset, hang to the boat, if you can, and hold up your legs. George, tell Pepe."

Ken backed the boat out from the shore. To his right in the middle of the narrow river was a racy current that he kept out of as long as possible. But presently he was drawn into it, and the boat shot forward, headed into the first incline, and went racing smoothly down toward the white waves of the rapids.

This was a trying moment for Ken. Grip as hard as he might, the oar-handles slipped in his sweaty hands.

The boys were yelling, but Ken could not hear for the din of roaring waters. The boat sailed down with a swift, gliding motion. When it thumped into the back-lash of the first big waves the water threshed around and over the boys. Then they were in the thick of rush and roar. Ken knew he was not handling the boat well. It grazed stones that should have been easy to avoid, and bumped on hidden ones, and got half broadside to the current. Pepe, by quick action with an oar, pushed the stern aside from collision with more than one rock. Several times Ken missed a stroke when a powerful one was needed. He passed between stones so close together that he had to ship the oars. It was all rapid water, this stretch, but the bad places, with sunken rocks, falls, and big waves, were strung out at such distances apart that Ken had time to get the boat going right before entering them.

Ken saw scarcely anything of the banks of the river. They blurred in his sight. Sometimes they were near, sometimes far. The boat turned corners where rocky ledges pointed out, constricting the stream and making

● ● ●

a curved channel. What lay around the curve was always a question and a cause for suspense. Often the boat raced down a chute and straight toward a rocky wall. Ken would pull back with all his might, and Pepe would break the shock by striking the wall with his oar.

More than once Pepe had a narrow escape from being knocked overboard. George tried to keep him from standing up. Finally at the end of a long rapid, Pepe, who had the stern-seat, jumped up and yelled. Ken saw a stone directly in the path of the boat, and he pulled back on the oars with a quick, strong jerk. Pepe shot out of the stern as if he had been flung from a catapult. He swam with the current while the boat drifted. He reached smooth water and the shore before Ken could pick him up.

It was fun for everybody but Ken. There were three inches of water in the boat. The canvas, however, had been arranged to protect guns, grips, and supplies. George had been wet before he entered the rapids, so a little additional water did not matter to him. Hal was almost as wet as Pepe.

"I'm glad that's past," said Ken.

With that long rapid behind him he felt different. It was what he had needed. His nervousness disappeared and he had no dread of the next fall. While the boys bailed out the boat Ken rested and thought. He had made mistakes in that rapid just passed. Luck had favored him. He went over the mistakes and saw where he had been wrong and how he could have avoided them if he had felt right. Ken realized now that this was a daredevil trip. And the daredevil in him had been shut up in dread. It took just that nervous dread, and the hard

IN THE WHITE WATER

● ● ●

work, blunders and accidents, the danger and luck, to liberate the spirit that would make the trip a success. Pepe and George were loud in their praises of Ken. But they did not appreciate the real hazard of the undertaking, and if Hal did he was too much of a wild boy to care.

"All aboard," called George.

Then they were on their way again. Ken found himself listening for rapids. It was no surprise to hear a dull roar round the next bend. His hair rose stiffly under his hat. But this time he did not feel the chill, the uncertainty, the lack of confidence that had before weakened him.

At the head of a long, shallow incline the boys tumbled overboard, Ken and Hal at the bow, Pepe and George at the stern. They waded with the bow upstream. The water tore around their legs, rising higher and higher. Soon Pepe and George had to climb in the boat, for the water became so deep and swift they could not wade.

"Jump in, Hal," called Ken.

Then he held to the bow an instant longer, wading a little farther down. This was ticklish business, and all depended upon Ken. He got the stern of the boat straight in line with the channel he wanted to run, then he leaped aboard and made for the oars. The boat sped down. At the bottom of this incline was a mass of leaping green and white waves. The blunt stern of the boat made a great splash and the water flew over the boys. They came through the roar and hiss and spray to glide into a mill-race current.

"Never saw such swift water!" exclaimed Ken.

• • •

This incline ended in a sudden plunge between two huge rocks. Ken saw the danger long before it became evident to his companions. There was no other way to shoot the rapid. He could not reach the shore. He must pass between the rocks. Ken pushed on one oar, then on the other, till he got the boat in line, and then he pushed with both oars. The boat flew down that incline. It went so swiftly that if it had hit one of the rocks it would have been smashed to kindling wood. Hal crouched low. George's face was white. And Pepe leaned forward with his big arms outstretched, ready to try to prevent a collision.

Down! Down with the speed of the wind! The boat flashed between the black stones. Then it was raised aloft, light as a feather, to crash into the backlashers. The din deafened Ken; the spray blinded him. The boat seemed to split a white pall of water, then, with many a bounce, drifted out of that rapid into little choppy waves, and from them into another long, smooth runway.

Ken rested and had nothing to say. Pepe shook his black head. Hal looked at his brother. George had forgotten his rifle. No one spoke.

Soon Ken had more work on hand. For round another corner lay more fast water. The boat dipped on a low fall, and went down into the midst of green waves with here and there ugly rocks splitting the current. The streambed was continually new and strange to Ken, and he had never seen such queer formations of rock. This rapid, however, was easy to navigate. A slanting channel of swift water connected it with another rapid. Ken backed into that one, passed through, only to face an-

• • •

other. And so it went for a long succession of shallow rapids.

A turn in the winding lane of cypresses revealed walls of gray, between which the river disappeared.

"Aha!" muttered Ken.

"Ken, I'll bet this is the place you've been looking for," said Hal.

The absence of any roar of water emboldened Ken. Nearing the head of the ravine, he stood upon the seat and looked ahead. But Ken could not see many rods ahead. The ravine turned, and it was the deceiving turns in the river that he had feared. What a strange sensation Ken had when he backed the boat into the mouth of that gorge! He was forced against his will. Yet there seemed to be a kind of blood-tingling pleasure in the prospect.

The current caught the boat and drew it between the gray-green walls of rock.

"It's coming to us," said the doubtful George.

The current ran all of six miles an hour. This was not half as fast as the boys had traveled in rapids, but it appeared swift enough because of the nearness of the over-shadowing walls. In the shade the water took on a different coloring. It was brown and oily. It slid along silently. It was deep, and the swirling current suggested power. Here and there long, creeping ferns covered the steep stone sides, and above ran a stream of blue sky fringed by leaning palms. Once Hal put his hands to his lips and yelled: "Hel-lo!" The yell seemed to rip the silence and began to clap from wall to wall. It gathered quickness until it clapped in one fiendish rattle. Then it wound away from the passage, growing fainter and fainter, and at last died in a hollow echo.

KEN WARD IN THE JUNGLE

● ● ●

"Don't do that again," ordered Ken.

He began to wish he could see the end of that gorge. But it grew narrower, and the shade changed to twilight, and there were no long, straight stretches. The river kept turning corners. Quick to note the slightest change in conditions, Ken felt a breeze, merely a zephyr, fan his hot face. The current had almost imperceptibly quickened. Yet it was still silent. Then on the gentle wind came a low murmur. Ken's pulse beat fast. Turning his ear downstream, he strained his hearing. The low murmur ceased. Perhaps he had imagined it. Still he kept listening. There! Again it came, low, far away, strange. It might have been the wind in the palms. But no, he could not possibly persuade himself it was wind. And as that faint breeze stopped he lost the sound once more. The river was silent, and the boat, and the boys—it was a silent ride. Ken divined that his companions were enraptured. But this ride had no beauty, no charm for him.

There! Another faint puff of wind, and again the low murmur! He fancied it was louder. He was beginning to feel an icy dread when all was still once more. So the boat drifted swiftly on with never a gurgle of water about her gunwales. The river gleamed in brown shadows. Ken saw bubbles rise and break on the surface, and there was a slight rise or swell of the water toward the center of the channel. This bothered him. He could not understand it. But then there had been many other queer formations of rock and freaks of current along this river.

The boat glided on and turned another corner, the sharpest one yet. A long, shadowy water-lane, walled in

IN THE WHITE WATER

● ● ●

to the very skies, opened up to Ken's keen gaze. The water here began to race onward, still wonderfully silent. And now the breeze carried a low roar. It was changeable yet persistent. It deepened.

Once more Ken felt his hair rise under his hat. Cold sweat wet his skin. Despite the pounding of his heart and the throb of his veins, his blood seemed to clog, to freeze, to stand still.

That roar was the roar of rapids. Impossible to go back! If there had been four sets of oars, Ken and his comrades could not row the heavy boat back up that swift, sliding river.

They must go on.

10

Lost!

●

"Ken, old man, do you hear that?" questioned Hal, waking from his trance.

George likewise rose out of his lazy contentment. "Must be rapids," he muttered. "If we strike rapids in this gorge it's all day with us. What did I tell you!"

Pepe's dark, searching eyes rested on Ken.

But Ken had no word for any of them. He was fighting an icy numbness, and the weakness of muscle and the whirl of his mind. It was thought of responsibility that saved him from collapse.

"It's up to you, old man," said Hal, quietly.

In a moment like this the boy could not wholly be deceived.

Ken got a grip upon himself. He looked down the long, narrow lane of glancing water. Some hundred yards on, it made another turn round a corner, and from

• • •

this dim curve came the roar. The current was hurrying the boat toward it, but not fast enough to suit Ken. He wanted to see the worst, to get into the thick of it, to overcome it. So he helped the boat along. A few moments sufficed to cover that gliding stretch of river, yet to Ken it seemed never to have an end. The roar steadily increased. The current became still stronger. Ken saw eruptions of water rising as from an explosion beneath the surface. Whirlpools raced along with the boat. The dim, high walls re-echoed the roaring of the water.

The first thing Ken saw when he sailed round that corner was a widening of the chasm and bright sunlight ahead. Perhaps an eighth of a mile below the steep walls ended abruptly. Next, in a quick glance he saw a narrow channel of leaping, tossing, curling white-crested waves under sunlighted mist and spray.

Pulling powerfully back and to the left Ken brought the boat alongside the cliff. Then he shipped his oars.

"Hold hard," he yelled, and he grasped the stone. The boys complied, and thus stopped the boat. Ken stood up on the seat. It was a bad place he looked down into, but he could not see any rocks. And rocks were what he feared most.

"Hold tight, boys," he said. Then he got Pepe to come to him and sit on the seat. Ken stepped up on Pepe's shoulders and, by holding to the rock, was able to get a good view of the rapid. It was not a rapid at all, but a constriction of the channel, and also a steep slant. The water rushed down so swiftly to get through that it swelled in the center in a long frothy ridge of waves. The water was deep. Ken could not see any bumps or splits or white-wreathed rocks, such as were conspicu-

● ● ●

ous in a rapid. The peril here for Ken was to let the boat
hit the wall or turn broadside or get out of that long
swelling ridge.

He stepped down and turned to the white-faced boys.
He had to yell close to them to make them hear him in
the roar.

"I—can—run—this—place. But—you've got—to
help. Pull—the canvas—up higher in the stern—and
hold it."

Then he directed Pepe to kneel in the bow of the boat
with an oar and be ready to push off from the walls.

If Ken had looked again or hesitated a moment he
would have lost his nerve. He recognized that fact. And
he shoved off instantly. Once the boat had begun to
glide down, gathering momentum, he felt his teeth grind
hard and his muscles grow tense. He had to bend his
head from side to side to see beyond the canvas George
and Hal were holding round their shoulders. He believed with that acting as a buffer in the stern he could
go pounding through those waves. Then he was in the
middle of the channel, and the boat fairly sailed along.
Ken kept his oars poised, ready to drop either one for a
stroke. All he wanted was to enter those foaming, tu-
multuous waves with his boat pointed right. He knew
he could not hope to see anything low down after he entered the race. He calculated that the last instant would
give him an opportunity to get his direction in line with
some object.

Then, even as he planned it, the boat dipped on a
beautiful glassy incline, and glided down toward the en-
gulfing, roaring waves. Above them, just in the center,

● ● ●

Ken caught sight of the tufted top of a palm tree. That was his landmark!

The boat shot into a great, curling, backlashing wave. There was a heavy shock, a pause, and then Ken felt himself lifted high, while a huge fan-shaped sheet of water rose behind the buffer in the stern. Walls and sky and trees faded under a watery curtain. Then the boat shot on again; the light came, the sky shone, and Ken saw his palm tree. He pulled hard on the right oar to get the stern back in line. Another heavy shock, a pause, a blinding shower of water, and then the downward rush! Ken got a fleeting glimpse of his guiding mark, and sunk the left oar deep for a strong stroke. The beating of the waves upon the upraised oars almost threw him out of the boat. The wrestling waters hissed and bellowed. Down the boat shot and up, to pound and pound, and then again shoot down. Through the pall of mist and spray Ken always got a glimpse, quick as lightning, of the palm tree, and like a demon he plunged in his oars to keep the boat in line. He was only dimly conscious of the awfulness of the place. But he was not afraid. He felt his action as being inspirited by something grim and determined. He was fighting the river.

All at once a grating jar behind told him the bow had hit a stone or a wall. He did not dare look back. The most fleeting instant of time might be the one for him to see his guiding mark. Then the boat lurched under him, lifted high with bow up, and lightened. He knew Pepe had been pitched overboard.

In spite of the horror of the moment, Ken realized that the lightening of the boat made it more buoyant, easier to handle. That weight in the bow had given him an unbalanced craft. But now one stroke here and one there kept the stern straight. The palm tree loomed higher and closer through the brightening mist. Ken no longer felt the presence of the walls. The thunderous roar had begun to lose some of its volume. Then with a crash through a lashing wave the boat raced out into the open light. Ken saw a beautiful foam-covered pool, down toward which the boat kept bumping over a succession of diminishing waves.

He gave a start of joy to see Pepe's black head bobbing in the choppy channel. Pepe had beat the boat to the outlet. He was swimming easily, and evidently he had not been injured.

Ken turned the bow toward him. But Pepe did not need any help, and a few more strokes put him in shallow water. Ken discovered that the boat, once out of the current, was exceedingly loggy and hard to row. It was half full of water. Ken's remaining strength went to pull ashore, and there he staggered out and dropped on the rocky bank.

The blue sky was very beautiful and sweet to look at just then. But Ken had to close his eyes. He did not have strength left to keep them open. For a while all seemed dim and obscure to him. Then he felt a dizziness, which in turn succeeded to a racing riot of his nerves and veins. His heart gradually resumed a normal beat, and his bursting lungs seemed to heal. A sickening languor lay upon him. He could not hold little stones which he felt under his fingers. He could not raise his hands. The life appeared to have gone from his legs.

All this passed, at length, and, hearing Hal's voice, Ken sat up. The outfit was drying in the sun; Pepe was

● ● ●

bailing out the boat; George was wiping his guns; and Hal was nursing a very disheveled little racoon.

"You can bring on any old thing now, for all I care," said Hal. "I'd shoot Lachine Rapids with Ken at the oars."

"He's a fine boatman," replied George. "Weren't you scared when we were in the middle of that darned place?"

"Me? Naw!"

"Well, I was scared, and don't you forget it," said Ken to them.

"You were all in, Ken," replied Hal. "Never saw you so tuckered out. The day you and Prince went after the cougar along that cañon precipice—you were all in that time. George, it took Ken six hours to climb out of that hole."

"Tell me about it," said George, all eyes.

"No stories now," put in Ken. "The sun is still high. We've got to be on our way. Let's look over the lay of the land."

Below the pool was a bold, rocky bluff, round which the river split. What branch to take was a matter of doubt and anxiety to Ken. Evidently this bluff was an island. It had a yellow front and long bare ledges leading into the river.

Ken climbed the bluff, accompanied by the boys, and found it covered with palm trees. Up there everything was so dry and hot that it did not seem to be jungle at all. Even the palms were yellow and parched. Pepe stood the heat, but the others could not endure it. Ken took one long look at the surrounding country, so wild and dry and still, and then led the way down the loose, dusty shelves.

Thereupon he surveyed the right branch of the river and followed it a little distance. The stream here foamed and swirled among jagged rocks. At the foot of this rapid stretched the first dead water Ken had encountered for miles. A flock of wild geese rose from under his feet and flew downstream.

"Geese!" exclaimed Ken. "I wonder if that means we are getting down near lagoons or big waters. George, wild geese don't frequent little streams, do they?"

"There's no telling where you'll find them in this country," answered George. "I've chased them right in our orange groves."

They returned to look at the left branch of the river. It was open and one continuous succession of low steps. That would have decided Ken even if the greater volume of water had not gone down on this left side. As far as he could see was a wide, open river running over little ledges. It looked to be the easiest and swiftest navigation he had come upon, and so indeed it proved. The water was swift, and always dropped over some ledge in a rounded fall that was safe for him to shoot. It was great fun going over these places. The boys hung their feet over the gunwales most of the time, sliding them along the slippery ledge or giving a kick to help the momentum. When they came to a fall, Ken would drop off the bow, hold the boat back and swing it straight, then jump in, and over it would go—souse!

There were so many of these ledges, and they were so close together, that going over them grew to be a habit. It induced carelessness. The boat drifted to the

LOST!

• • •

brow of a fall full four feet high. Ken, who was at the bow, leaped off just in time to save the boat. He held on while the swift water surged about his knees. He yelled for the boys to jump. As the stern where they sat was already over the fall it was somewhat difficult to make the boys vacate quickly enough.

"Tumble out! Quick!" bawled Ken. "Do you think I'm Samson?"

Over they went, up to their necks in the boiling foam, and not a second too soon, for Ken could hold the boat no longer. It went over smoothly, just dipping the stern under water. If the boys had remained aboard, the boat would have swamped. As it was, Pepe managed to catch the rope, which Ken had wisely thrown out, and he drifted down to the next ledge. Ken found this nearly as high as the last one. So he sent the boys below to catch the boat. This worked all right. The shelves slanted slightly, with the shallow part of the water just at the break of the ledge. They passed half a dozen of these, making good time, and before they knew it were again in a deep, smooth jungle lane with bamboo and streamers of moss waving over them.

The shade was cool, and Ken settled down in the stern-seat, grateful for a rest. To his surprise, he did not see a bird. The jungle was asleep. Once or twice Ken fancied he heard the tinkle and gurgle of water running over rocks. The boat glided along silently, with Pepe rowing leisurely, George asleep, Hal dreaming.

Ken watched the beautiful green banks. They were high, a mass of big-leaved vines, flowering and fragrant, above which towered the jungle giants. Ken wanted to get out and study those forest trees. But he

• • •

made no effort to act upon his good intentions, and felt that he must make the most of his forestry study at long range. He was reveling in the cool recesses under the leaning cypresses, in the soft swish of bearded moss, and the strange rustle of palms, in the dreamy hum of the resting jungle, when his pleasure was brought to an abrupt end.

"Santa Maria!" yelled Pepe.

George woke up with a start. Hal had been jarred out of his day-dream, and looked resentful. Ken gazed about him with the feeling of a man going into a trance, instead of coming out of one.

The boat was fast on a mud bank. That branch of the river ended right there. The boys had come all those miles to run into a blind pocket.

Ken's glance at the high yellow bank, here crumbling and bare, told him there was no outlet. He had a sensation of blank dismay.

"Gee!" exclaimed Hal, softly.

George rubbed his eyes, and, searching for a cigarette, he muttered: "We're lost! I said it was coming to us. We've got to go back!"

11

An Army of Snakes

•

For a moment Ken Ward was utterly crushed under the weight of this sudden blow. It was so sudden that he had no time to think; or his mind was clamped on the idea of attempting to haul the boat up that long, insurmountable series of falls.

"It'll be an awful job," burst out Hal.

No doubt in the mind of each boy was the same idea—the long haul, wading over slippery rocks; the weariness of pushing legs against the swift current; the packing of supplies uphill; and then the toil of lifting the heavy boat up over a fall.

"Mucho malo," said Pepe, and he groaned. That was significant, coming from a *mozo*, who thought nothing of rowing forty miles in a day.

"Oh, but it's tough luck," cried Ken. "Why didn't I choose the right branch of this pesky river?"

• • •

"I think you used your head at that," said Hal. "Most of the water came down on this side. Where did it go?"

Hal had hit the vital question, and it cleared Ken's brain.

"Hal, you're talking sense. Where did that water go? It couldn't all have sunk into the earth. We'll find out. We won't try to go back. We *can't* go back."

Pepe shoved off the oozy mud, and, reluctantly, as if he appreciated the dilemma, he turned the boat and rowed along the shore. As soon as Ken had recovered somewhat he decided there must be an outlet which he had missed. This reminded him that at a point not far back he had heard the tinkle and gurgle of unseen water flowing over rocks.

He directed Pepe to row slowly along the bank that he thought was the island side. As they glided under the drooping bamboos and silky curtains of moss George began to call out: "Low bridge! Low bridge!" For a boy who was forever voicing ill-omened suggestions as to what might soon happen he was extraordinarily cheerful.

There were places where all had to lie flat and others where Pepe had to use his *machete*. This disturbed the *siesta* of many aquatic birds, most of which flew swiftly away. But there were many of the gray-breasted, blue-backed bitterns that did not take to flight. These croaked dismally, and looked down upon the boys with strange, protruding eyes.

"Those darn birds'll give me the willies," declared Hal. "George, you look just like them when you croak about what's coming to us."

AN ARMY OF SNAKES

● ● ●

"Just wait!" retorted George. "It'll come, all right. Then I'll have the fun of seeing you scared silly."

"What! You'll not do anything of the kind!" cried Hal, hotly. "I've been in places where such—such a skinny little sap-head as you—"

"Here, you kids stop wrangling," ordered Ken, who sensed hostilities in the air. "We've got trouble enough."

Suddenly Ken signaled Pepe to stop rowing.

"Boys, I hear running water. Aha! Here's a current. See—it's making right under this bank."

Before them was a high wall of broad-leaved vines, so thick that nothing could be seen through them. Apparently this luxuriant canopy concealed the bank. Pepe poked an oar into it, but found nothing solid.

"Pepe, cut a way through. We've got to see where this water runs."

It was then that Ken came to a full appreciation of a *machete*. He had often fancied it a much less service-able tool than an ax. Pepe flashed the long, bright blade up, down, and around, and presently the boat was its own length in a green tunnel. Pepe kept on slashing while Ken poled the boat in and the other boys dumped the cut foliage overboard. Soon they got through this mass of hanging vine and creeper. Much to Ken's surprise and delight, he found no high bank, but low, flat ground, densely wooded, through which ran a narrow, deep outlet of the river.

"By all that's lucky!" ejaculated Ken.

George and Hal whooped their pleasure, and Pepe rubbed his muscular hands. Then all fell silent. The

● ● ●

deep, penetrating silence of that jungle was not provoc-
ative of speech. The shade was so black that when a ray
of sunlight did manage to pierce the dense canopy overhead it resembled a brilliant golden spear. A few lofty
palms and a few clumps of bamboo rather emphasized
the lack of these particular species in this forest. Nor
was there any of the familiar streaming moss hanging
from the trees. This glen was green, cool, dark. It did
not smell exactly swampy, but rank, like a place where
many water plants were growing.

The outlet was so narrow that Ken was not able to
use the oars. Still, as the current was swift, the boat
went along rapidly. He saw a light ahead and heard the
babble of water. The current quickened, and the boat
drifted suddenly upon the edge of an oval glade, where
the hot sun beat down. A series of abrupt mossy
benches, over which the stream slid almost noiselessly,
blocked further progress.

The first thing about this glade that Ken noted particularly, after the difficulties presented by the steep steps,
was the multitude of snakes sunning themselves along
the line of further progress.

"Boys, it'll be great wading down there, hey?" he
queried.

Pepe grumbled for the first time on the trip. Ken
gathered from the native's looks and speech that he did
not like snakes.

"Watch me peg 'em!" yelled Hal, and he began to
throw stones with remarkable accuracy. "Hike, you
brown sons-of-guns!"

George, not to be outdone, made a dive for his .22

AN ARMY OF SNAKES

● ● ●

and began to pop as if he had no love for snakes. Ken had doubts about this species. The snakes were short, thick, dull brown in color, and the way they slipped into the stream proved they were water-snakes. Ken had never read of a brown water-moccasin, so he doubted that these belonged to that poisonous family. Anyway, snakes were the least of his troubles.

"Boys, you're doing fine," he said. "There are about a thousand snakes there, and you've hit about six."

He walked down through the glade into the forest, and was overjoyed to hear once more the heavy roar of rapids. He went on. The timber grew thinner, and light penetrated the jungle. Presently he saw the gleam of water through the trees. Then he hurried back.

"All right, boys," he shouted. "Here's the river."

The boys were so immensely relieved that packing the outfit round the waterfalls was work they set about with alacrity. Ken, who had on his boots, broke a trail through the ferns and deep moss. Pepe, being barefoot, wasted time looking for snakes. George teased him. But Pepe was deadly serious. And the way he stepped and looked made Ken thoughtful. He had made his last trip with supplies, and was about to start back to solve the problem of getting the boat down, when a hoarse yell resounded through the sleeping jungle. Parrots screeched, and other birds set up a cackling.

Ken bounded up the slope.

"Santa Maria!" cried Pepe.

KEN WARD IN THE JUNGLE

● ● ●

Ken followed the direction indicated by Pepe's staring eyes and trembling finger. Hanging from a limb of a tree was a huge black-snake. It was as thick as Ken's leg. The branch upon which it poised its neck so gracefully was ten feet high, and the tail curled into the ferns on the ground.

"Boys, it's one of the big fellows," cried Ken.

"Didn't I tell you!" yelled George, running down for his gun.

Hal seemed rooted to the spot. Pepe began to jabber. Ken watched the snake, and felt instinctively from its sinister looks that it was dangerous. George came running back with his .32 and waved it in the air as he shot. He was so frightened that he forgot to aim. Ken took the rifle from him.

"You can't hit him with this. Run after your shotgun. Quick!"

But the sixteen-gauge was clogged with a shell that would not eject. Ken's guns were in their cases.

"Holy smoke!" cried George. "He's coming down."

The black-snake moved his body and began to slide toward the tree trunk.

Ken shot twice at the head of the snake. It was a slow-swaying mark hard to hit. The reptile stopped and poised wonderfully on the limb. He was not coiled about it, but lay over it with about four feet of neck waving, swaying to and fro. He watched the boys, and his tongue, like a thin, black streak, darted out viciously.

Ken could not hit the head, so he sent a bullet through the thick part of the body. Swift as a gleam the snake darted from the limb.

106

AN ARMY OF SNAKES

• • •

"Santa Maria!" yelled Pepe, and he ran off.

"Look out, boys," shouted Ken. He picked up Pepe's *machete* and took to his heels. George and Hal scrambled before him. They ran a hundred yards or more, and Ken halted in an open rocky spot. He was angry, and a little ashamed that he had run. The snake did not pursue, and probably was as badly frightened as the boys had been. Pepe stopped some distance away, and Hal and George came cautiously back.

"I don't see anything of him," said Ken. "I'm going back."

He walked slowly, keeping a sharp outlook, and, returning to the glade, found bloodstains under the tree. The snake had disappeared without leaving a trail.

"If I'd had my shotgun ready!" exclaimed Ken, in disgust. And he made a note that in the future he would be prepared to shoot.

"Wasn't he a whopper, Ken?" said Hal. "We ought to have got his hide. What a fine specimen!"

"Boys, you drive away those few little snakes while I figure on a way to get the boat down."

"Not on your life!" replied Hal.

George ably sustained Hal's objection.

"Mucho malo," said Pepe, and then added a loud "No" in English.

"All right, my brave comrades," rejoined Ken, scornfully. "As I've not done any work yet or taken any risks, I'll drive the snakes away."

With Pepe's *machete* he cut a long forked pole, trimmed it, and, armed with this weapon, he assaulted the rolls and bands and balls of brown snakes. He stalked boldly down upon them, pushed and poled, and even kicked them off the mossy banks. Hal could not stand that, and presently he got a pole and went to Ken's assistance.

"Who's hollering now?" he yelled to George.

Whereupon George cut a long branch and joined the battle. They whacked and threshed and pounded, keeping time with yells. Everywhere along the wet benches slipped and splashed the snakes. But after they were driven into the water they did not swim away. They dove under the banks and then stretched out their pointed heads from the dripping edge of moss.

"Say, fellows, we're making it worse for us," declared Ken. "See, the brown devils won't swim off. We'd better have left them on the bank. Let's catch one and see if he'll bite."

He tried to pick up one on his pole, but it slipped off. George fished after another. Hal put the end of his stick down inside the coil of still another and pitched it. The brown, wriggling, wet snake shot straight at the unsuspecting George, and struck him and momentarily wound about him.

"Augrrh!" bawled George, flinging off the reptile and leaping back. "What'd you do that for? I'll punch you!"

"George, he didn't mean it," said Ken. "It was an accident. Come on, let's tease that fellow and see if he'll bite."

The snake coiled and raised his flat head and darted a wicked tongue out and watched with bright, beady eyes, but he did not strike. Ken went as close as he thought safe and studied the snake.

"Boys, his head isn't a triangle, and there are no little pits under his eyes. Those are two signs of a poisonous snake. I don't believe this fellow's one."

"He'll be a dead snake, b'gosh," replied George, and he fell to pounding it with his pole.

"Don't smash him. I want the skin," yelled Hal.

Ken pondered on the situation before him.

"Come, the sooner we get at this the better," he said.

There was a succession of benches through which the stream zigzagged and tumbled. These benches were rock ledges over which moss had grown fully a foot thick, and they were so oozy and slippery that it was no easy task to walk upon them. Then they were steep, so steep that it was remarkable how the water ran over them so smoothly, with very little noise or break. It was altogether a new kind of waterfall to Ken. But if the snakes had not been hidden there, navigation would have presented an easier problem.

"Come on boys, alongside now, and hold back," he ordered, gripping the bow.

Exactly what happened in the next few seconds was not clear in his mind. There was a rush, and all were being dragged by the boat. The glade seemed to whizz past. There were some sodden thumps, a great splashing, a check—and lo! they were over several benches. It was the quickest and easiest descent he had ever made down a steep waterfall.

"Fine!" ejaculated George.

"Yes, it was fine," Ken replied. "But unless this boat has wings something'll happen soon."

Below was a long, swift curve of water, very narrow and steep, with a moss-covered rock dividing the lower end. Ken imagined if there was a repetition of the first descent, the boat would be smashed on that rock. He ordered Pepe, who was of course the strongest, to go below and jump to the rock. There he might prevent a collision.

Pepe obeyed, but as he went he yelled and doubled up in contortions as he leaped over snakes in the moss.

Then gently, gingerly the boys started the boat off the bench, where it had lodged. George was at the stern, Ken and Hal at the bow. Suddenly Hal shrieked and jumped straight up, to land in the boat.

"Snakes!" he howled.

"Give us a rest!" cried Ken, in disgust.

The boat moved as if by its own instinct. It dipped, then—*wheeze!* it dove over the bench. Hal was thrown off his feet, fell back on the gunwale, and thence into the snaky moss. George went sprawling face downward into the slimy ooze, and Ken was jerked clear off the bench into the stream. He got his footing and stood firm in water to his waist, and he had the bow-rope coiled round his hands.

"Help! Help!" he yelled, as he felt the dragging weight too much for him.

If Ken retarded the progress of the boat at all, it was not much. George saw his distress and the danger menacing the boat, and he leaped valiantly forward. As he dashed down a slippery slant his feet flew up higher than where his head had been; he actually turned over in the air and fell with a great sop.

Hal had been trying to reach Ken, but here he stopped and roared with laughter.

Despite Ken's anger and fear of snakes, and his greater fear for the boat, he likewise had to let out a peal of laughter. That tumble of George's was great. Then Ken's footing gave way and he went down. His mouth filled with nasty water, nearly strangling him. He was almost blinded, too. His arms seemed to be wrenched out of their sockets, and he felt himself bumping over moss-covered rocks as soft as cushions. Slimy ropes or roots of vegetation that felt like snakes brushed his face and made him cold and sick. It was impossible to hold the boat any longer. He lodged against a stone, and the swift water forced him upon it. Blinking and coughing, he stuck fast.

Ken saw the boat headed like a dart for the rock where Pepe stood.

"Let'er go!" yelled Ken. "Don't try to stop her. Pepe, you'll be smashed!"

Pepe acted like a man determined to make up for past cowardice. He made a great show of brave intentions. He was not afraid of a boat. He braced himself and reached out with his brawny arms. Ken feared for the obstinate native's life, for the boat moved with remarkable velocity.

At the last second Pepe's courage vanished. He turned tail to get out of the way. But he slipped. The boat shot toward him and the blunt stern struck him with a dull thud. Pepe sailed into the air, over the rock, and went down cleaving the water.

The boat slipped over the stone as easily as if it had been a wave and, gliding into still water below, lodged on the bank.

Ken crawled out of the stream, and when he ascertained that no one was injured he stretched himself on the ground and gave up to mirth. Pepe resembled a drowned rat; Hal was an object to wonder at; and George, in his coating of slime and with strings of moss in his hair, was the funniest thing Ken had ever seen. It was somewhat of a surprise to him to discover, presently, that the boys were convulsed with fiendish glee over the way he himself looked.

By and by they recovered, and, with many a merry jest and chuckle of satisfaction, they repacked the boat and proceeded on their way. No further obstacle hindered them. They drifted out of the shady jungle into the sunlit river.

In half a mile of drifting the heat of the sun dried the boys' clothes. The water was so hot that it fairly steamed. Once more the boat entered a placid aisle over which the magnificent gray-wreathed cypresses bowed, and the west wind waved long ribbons of moss, and wild fowl winged reluctant flight.

Ken took advantage of this tranquil stretch of river to work on his map. He realized that he must use every spare moment and put down his drawings and notes as often as time and travel permitted. It had dawned on Ken that rapids and snakes, and all the dangers along the river, made his task of observation and study one

• • •

apt to be put into eclipse at times. Once or twice he landed on shore to climb a bluff, and was pleased each time to see that he had lined a comparatively true course on his map. He had doubts of its absolute accuracy, yet he could not help having pride in his work. So far so good, he thought, and hoped for good fortune farther down the river.

12

Catching Strange Fish

●

Beyond a bend in the river the boys came upon an island with a narrow, shaded channel on one side, a wide shoal on the other, and a group of huge cypresses at the upstream end.

"Looks good to me," said Hal.

The instant Ken saw the island he knew it was the place he had long been seeking to make a permanent camp for a few days. They landed, to find an ideal camping site. The ground under the cypresses was flat, dry, and covered with short grass. Not a ray of sunlight penetrated the foliage. A pile of driftwood had lodged against one of the trees, and this made easy the question of firewood.

"Great!" exclaimed Ken. "Come on, let's look over the ground.

The island was about two hundred yards long, and

● ● ●

the lower end was hidden by a growth of willows. Bursting through this, the boys saw a weedy flat leading into a wide, shallow back-eddy. Great numbers of ducks were sporting and feeding. The stones of the rocky shore were lined with sleeping ducks. Herons of all colors and sizes waded about or slept on one leg. Snipe ran everywhere. There was a great squawking and flapping of wings. But at least half the number of water-fowl were too tame or too lazy to fly.

Ken returned to camp with his comrades, all highly elated over the prospects. The best feature about this beautiful island was the absence of ticks and snakes.

"Boys, this is the place," said Ken. "We'll hang up here for a while. Maybe we won't strike another such nice place to stay."

So they unloaded the boat, taking everything out, and proceeded to pitch a camp that was a delight. They were all loud in expressions of satisfaction. Then Pepe set about leisurely peeling potatoes; George took his gun and slipped off toward the lower end of the island; Hal made a pen for his racoon, and then more pens, as if he meant to capture a menagerie; and Ken made a comfortable lounging-bed under a cypress. He wanted to forget that nagging worry as to the farther descent of the river and to enjoy this place.

"Bang!" went George's sixteen-gauge. A loud whirring of wings followed, and the air was full of ducks.

"Never touched one!" yelled Hal, in taunting voice.

A flock of teal skimmed the water and disappeared upstream. The shot awakened parrots in the trees, where for a while there was clamor. Ken saw George wade out into the shoal and pick up three ducks.

• • •

"Pot-shot!" exclaimed Hal, disgustedly. "Why couldn't he be a sport and shoot them on the fly?"

George crossed to the opposite shore and, climbing a bare place, stood looking before him.

"Hey, George, don't go far," called Ken.

"Fine place over here," replied George, and, waving his hand, he passed into the bushes out of sight.

Ken lay back upon his blanket with a blissful sense of rest and contentment. Many a time he had lain so, looking up through the broad leaves of a sycamore or the lacy foliage of a birch or the delicate crisscross of millions of pine needles. This overhead canopy, however, was different. Only here and there could he catch little slivers of blue sky. The graceful streamers of exquisite moss hung like tassels of silver. In the dead stillness of noonday they seemed to float curved in the shape in which the last soft breeze had left them. High upon a branch he saw a red-headed parrot hanging back downward, after the fashion of a monkey. Then there were two parrots asleep in the fork of a branch. It was the middle of the day, and all things seemed tired and sleepy. The deep channel murmured drowsily, and the wide expanse of river on the other side lapped lazily at the shore. The only other sound was the mourning of turtle-doves, one near and another far away. Again the full richness, the mellow sweetness of this song struck Ken forcibly. He remembered that all the way down the river he had heard that mournful note. It was beautiful but melancholy. Somehow it made him think that it had broken the dreamy stillness of the jungle noonday long, long ago. It was sweet but sad and old. He did not like to hear it.

CATCHING STRANGE FISH

● ● ●

Ken yielded to the soothing influence of the hour and fell asleep. When he awoke there was George, standing partially undressed and very soberly popping ticks. He had enlisted the services of Pepe, and, to judge from the remarks of both, they needed still more assistance.

"Say, Garrapato George, many ticks over there?"

"Ticks!" shouted George, wildly, waving his cigarette. "Millions of 'em! And there's—ouch! Kill that one, Pepe. Wow! he's as big as a penny. There's game over there. It's a flat with some kind of berry bush. There's lots of trails. I saw cat tracks, and I scared up wild turkeys—"

"Turkeys!" Ken exclaimed, eagerly.

"You bet. I saw a dozen. How they can run! I didn't flush them. Then I saw a flock of those black and white ducks, like the big fellow I shot. They were feeding. I believe they're Muscovy ducks."

"I'm sure I don't know, but we can call them that."

"Well, I'd got a shot, too, but I saw some gray things sneaking in the bushes. I thought they were pigs, so I got out of there quick."

"You mean javelin?"

"Yep, I mean wild pigs. Oh! We've struck the place for game. I'll bet it's coming to us."

When George anticipated pleasurable events he was the most happy of companions. It was good to look forward. He was continually expecting things to happen; he was always looking ahead with great eagerness. But unfortunately he had a twist of mind toward the unfavorable side of events, and so always had the boys fearful.

"Well, pigs or no pigs, ticks or no ticks, we'll hunt

and fish, and see all there is to see," declared Ken, and he went back to his lounging.

When he came out of that lazy spell, George and Hal were fishing. George had Ken's rod, and it happened to be the one Ken thought most of.

"Do you know how to fish?" he asked.

"I've caught tarpon bigger'n you," retorted George.

That fact was indeed too much for Ken, and he had nothing to do but risk his beloved rod in George's hands. And the way George swung it about, slashed branches with it, dropped the tip in the water, was exceedingly alarming to Ken. The boy would break the tip in a minute. Yet Ken could not take his rod away from a boy who had caught tarpon.

There were fish breaking water. Where a little while before the river had been smooth, now it was ruffled by *ravalo*, gar, and other fish Pepe could not name. But George and Hal did not get a bite. They tried all their artificial flies and spoons and minnows, then the preserved mullet, and finally several kinds of meat.

"Bah! they want pie," said Hal.

For Ken Ward to see little and big fish capering around under his very nose and not be able to hook one was exasperating. He shot a small fish, not unlike a pickerel, and had the boys bait with that. Still no strike was forthcoming.

This put Ken on his mettle. He rigged up a minnow tackle, and, going to the lower end of the island, he tried to catch some minnows. There were plenty of them in the shallow water, but they would not bite. Finally, Ken waded in the shoal and turned over stones.

CATCHING STRANGE FISH

● ● ●

He found some snails almost as large as mussels, and with these he hurried back to the boys.

"Here, if you don't get a bite on one of these I'm no fisherman," said Ken. "Try one."

George got his hands on the new bait in advance of Hal and so threw his hook into the water first. No sooner had the bait sunk than he got a strong pull.

"There! Careful now," said Ken.

George jerked up, hooking a fish that made the rod look like a buggy-whip.

"Give me the rod," yelled Ken, trying to take it.

"It's my fish," yelled back George.

He held on and hauled with all his might. A long, finely built fish, green as emerald, split the water and churned it into foam. Then, sweeping out in a strong dash, it broke Ken's rod square in the middle. Ken eyed the wreck with sorrow, and George with no little disapproval.

"You said you knew how to fish," protested Ken.

"Those split-bamboo rods are no good," replied George. "They won't hold a fish."

"George, you're a grand fisherman!" observed Hal, with a chuckle. "Why, you only dreamed you've caught tarpon."

Just then Hal had a tremendous strike. He was nearly hauled off the bank. But he recovered his balance and clung to his nodding rod. Hal's rod was heavy cane, and his line was thick enough to suit. So nothing broke. The little brass reel buzzed and rattled.

"I've got a whale!" yelled Hal.

"It's a big gar—alligator-gar," said George. "You haven't got him. He's got you."

KEN WARD IN THE JUNGLE

● ● ●

The fish broke water, showing long, open jaws with teeth like saw-teeth. It threshed about and broke away. Hal reeled in to find the hook straightened out. Then George kindly commented upon the very skilful manner in which Hal had handled the gar. For a wonder Hal did not reply.

By four o'clock, when Ken sat down to supper, he was so thirsty that his mouth puckered as dry as if he had been eating green persimmons. This matter of thirst had become serious. Twice each day Ken had boiled a pot of water, into which he mixed cocoa, sugar, and condensed milk, and begged the boys to drink that and nothing else. Nevertheless, Pepe and George, and occasionally Hal, would drink unboiled water. For this meal the boys had venison and duck, and canned vegetables and fruit, so they fared sumptuously.

Pepe pointed to a string of Muscovy ducks sailing up the river. George had a good shot at the tail end of the flock, and did not even loosen a feather. Then a line of cranes and herons passed over the island. When a small bunch of teal flew by, to be followed by several canvasbacks, Ken ran for his shotgun. It was a fine hammerless, a hard-shooting gun, and one Ken used for grouse-hunting. In his hurry he grasped a handful of the first shells he came to and, when he ran to the riverbank, found they were loads of small shot. He decided to try them anyhow.

While Pepe leisurely finished the supper, Ken and George and Hal sat on the bank watching for ducks. Just before the sun went down a hard wind blew, making difficult shooting. Every few moments ducks would whir by. George's gun missed fire often, and when it

120

● ● ●

did work all right, he missed the ducks. To Ken's surprise he found the load of small shot very deadly. He could sometimes reach a duck at eighty yards. The little brown ducks and teal he stopped as if they had hit a stone wall. He dropped a canvasback with the sheer dead plunge that he liked. Ken thought a crippled duck enough to make a hunter quit shooting. With six ducks killed, he decided to lay aside his gun for that time, when Pepe pointed down the river.

"Pato real," he said.

Ken looked eagerly and saw three of the big black ducks flying as high as the tree-tops and coming fast. Snapping a couple of shells in the gun, Ken stood ready. At the end of the island two of the ducks wheeled to the left, but the big leader came on like a thunderbolt. To Ken he made a canvasback seem slow. Ken caught him over the sights of the gun, followed him up till he was abreast and beyond; then, sweeping a little ahead of him, Ken pulled both triggers. The Muscovy swooped up and almost stopped in his flight while a cloud of black feathers puffed away on the wind. He sagged a little, recovered, and flew on as strong as ever. The small shot were not heavy enough to stop him.

"We'll need big loads for the Muscovies and the turkeys," said George.

"We've all sizes up to BB's," replied Ken. "George, let's take a walk over there where you saw the turkeys. It's early yet."

Then Pepe told George if they wanted to see game at that hour, the thing to do was to sit still in camp and watch the game come down to the river to drink. And he pointed downstream to a herd of small deer quietly walking out on the bar.

"After all the noise we made!" exclaimed Ken. "Well, this beats me. George, we'll stay right here and not shoot again tonight. I've an idea we'll see something worthwhile."

It was Pepe's idea, but Ken instantly saw its possibilities. There were no tributaries to the river or springs in that dry jungle, and, as manifestly the whole country abounded in game, it must troop down to the river in the cool of the evening to allay the hot day's thirst. The boys were perfectly situated for watching the dark bank on the channel side of the island as well as the open bars on the other. The huge cypresses cast shadows that even in daylight effectually concealed them. They put out the camp-fire and, taking comfortable seats in the folds of the great gnarled roots, began to watch and listen.

The vanguard of thirsty deer had prepared Ken for something remarkable, and he was in no wise disappointed. The trooping of deer down to the water's edge and the flight of wild fowl upstream increased in proportion to the gathering shadows of twilight. The deer must have got a scent, for they raised their long ears and stood still as statues, gazing across toward the upper end of the island. But they showed no fear. It was only when they had drunk their fill and wheeled about to go up the narrow trails over the bank that they showed uneasiness and haste. This made Ken wonder if they were fearful of being ambushed by jaguars. Soon the dark line of deer along the shore shaded into the darkness of night. Then Ken heard soft splashes and an

• • •

occasional patter of hard hoofs. The whir of wings had ceased.

A low exclamation from Pepe brought attention to interesting developments closer at hand.

"Javelin!" he whispered.

On the channel side of the island was impenetrable pitchy blackness. Ken tried to pierce it with straining eyes, but he could not even make out the shoreline that he knew was only ten yards distant. Still he could hear, and that was thrilling enough. Everywhere on this side, along the edge of the water and up the steep bank, were faint tickings of twigs and soft rustlings of leaves. Then there was a continuous sound, so low as to be almost inaudible, that resembled nothing Ken could think of so much as a long line of softly dripping water. It swelled in volume to a tiny roll, and ended in a sharp clicking on rocks and a gentle splashing in the water. A drove of *javelin* had come down to drink. Occasionally the glint of green eyes made the darkness all the more weird. Suddenly a long, piercing wail, a keen cry almost human, quivered into the silence.

"Panther!" Ken whispered, instantly, to the boys. It was a different cry from that of the lion of the *cañon*, but there was a strange wild note that betrayed the species. A stillness fell, dead as that of a subterranean cavern. Strain his ears as he might, Ken could not detect the slightest sound. It was as if no *javelin* or any other animals had come down to drink. That listening, palpitating moment seemed endless. What mystery of wildlife it meant, that silence following the cry of the panther! Then the jungle sounds recommenced—the swishing of water, the brushing in the thicket, stealthy

• • •

padded footsteps, the faint snapping of twigs. Some kind of a cat uttered an unearthly squall. Close upon this the clattering of deer up the bank on the other side rang out sharply. The deer were running, and the striking of the little hoofs ceased in short order. Ken listened intently. From far over the bank came a sound not unlike a cough—deep, hoarse, inexpressibly wild and menacing.

"Tigre!" cried Pepe, gripping Ken hard with both hands. He could feel him trembling. It showed how the native of the jungle-belt feared the jaguar.

Again the cough rasped out, nearer and louder this time. It was not a courage-provoking sound, and seemed on second thought more of a growl than a cough. Ken felt safe on the island; nevertheless, he took up his rifle.

"That's a tiger," whispered George. "I heard one once from the porch of the Alamitas hacienda."

A third time the jaguar told of his arrival upon the night scene. Ken was excited, and had a thrill of fear. He made up his mind to listen with clearer ears, but the cough or growl was not repeated.

Then a silence set in, so unbroken that it seemed haunted by the echoes of those wild jungle cries. Perhaps Ken had the haunting echoes in mind. He knew what had sent the deer away and stilled the splashings and creepings. It was the hoarse voice of the lord of the jungle.

Pepe and the boys, too, fell under the spell of the hour. They did not break the charm by talking. Giant fireflies accentuated the ebony blackness and a low hum of insects riveted the attention on the stillness. Ken could not understand why he was more thoughtful on this trip than he had ever been before. Somehow he felt immeasurably older. Probably that was because it had seemed necessary for him to act like a man, even if he was only a boy.

The black mantle of night lifted from under the cypresses, leaving a gloom that slowly paled. Through the dark foliage, low down over the bank, appeared the white tropical moon. Shimmering gleams chased the shadows across the ripples, and slowly the river brightened to a silver sheen.

A great peace fell upon the jungle world. How white, how wild, how wonderful! It only made the island more beautiful and lonely. The thought of leaving it gave Ken Ward a pang. Almost he wished he were a savage.

And he lay there thinking of the wild places that he could never see, where the sun shone, the wind blew, the twilight shadowed, the rain fell; where the colors and beauties changed with the passing hours; where myriad wild creatures preyed upon each other, and night never darkened but upon strife and death.

13

A Turkey-hunt

•

Upon awakening in the early morning Ken found his state one of huge enjoyment. He was still lazily tired, but the dead drag and ache had gone from his bones. A cool breeze wafted the mist from the river, breaking it up into clouds, between which streamed rosy shafts of sunlight. Woodsmoke from the fire Pepe was starting blew fragrantly over him. A hundred thousand birds seemed to be trying to burst their throats. The air was full of music. He lay still, listening to this melodious herald of the day till it ceased.

Then a flock of parrots approached and circled over the island, screeching like a band of flying imps. Presently they alighted in the cypresses, bending the branches to a breaking-point and giving the trees a spotted appearance of green and red. Pepe waved his hand toward another flock sweeping over.

A TURKEY-HUNT

• • •

"Parrakeets," he said.

These birds were a solid green, much smaller than the red-heads, with longer tails. They appeared wilder than the red-heads, and flew higher, circling the same way and screeching, but they did not alight. Other flocks sailed presently from all directions. The last one was a cloud of parrots, a shining green and yellow mass several acres in extent. They flew still higher than the parrakeets.

"Yellow-heads!" shouted George. "They're the big fellows, the talkers. If there ain't a million of 'em!"

The boys ate breakfast in a din that made conversation useless. The red-heads swooped down upon the island, and the two unfriendly species flew back and forth, manifestly trying to drive the boys off. The mist had blown away, the sun was shining bright, when the myriad of parrots, in large and small flocks, departed to other jungle haunts.

Pepe rowed across the wide shoal to the sand-bars. There in the soft ooze, among the hundreds of deer tracks, Ken found a jaguar track larger than his spread hand. It was different from a lion track, yet he could not distinguish just what the difference was. Pepe, who had accompanied the boys to carry the rifles and game, pointed to the track and said, vehemently:

"Tigre!" He pronounced it "tee-gray." And he added, "Grande!"

"Big he certainly is," Ken replied. "Boys, we'll kill this jaguar. We'll bait this drinking trail with a deer carcass and watch tonight."

Once upon the bank, Ken was surprised to see a wide stretch of comparatively flat land. It was covered with a

• • •

low vegetation, with here and there palm trees on the little ridges and bamboo clumps down in the swales. Beyond the flat rose the dark line of dense jungle. It was not clear to Ken why that low piece of ground was not overgrown with the matted thickets and vines and big trees characteristic of other parts of the jungle.

They struck into one of the trails, and had not gone a hundred paces when they espied a herd of deer. The grass and low bushes almost covered them. George handed his shotgun to Pepe and took his rifle.

"Shoot low," said Ken.

George pulled the trigger, and with the report a deer went down, but it was not the one Ken was looking at, nor the one at which he believed George had aimed. The rest of the herd bounded away, to disappear in a swale. Wading through bushes and grass, they found George's quarry, a small deer weighing perhaps sixty pounds. Pepe carried it over to the trail. Ken noted that he was exceedingly happy to carry the rifles. They went on at random, somehow feeling that, no matter in what direction, they would run into something to shoot at.

The first bamboo swale was alive with *chicalocki*. Up to this time Ken had not seen this beautiful pheasant fly in the open, and he was astonished at its speed. It would burst out of the thick bamboo, whir its wings swiftly, then sail. That sail was a most graceful thing to see. George pulled his 16-gauge twice, and missed both times. He had the beginner's fault—shooting too soon. Presently Pepe beat a big cock *chicalocki* out of the bush. He made such a fine target, he sailed so evenly, that Ken simply looked at him over the gun-sights and followed him till he was out of sight. The next one he

A TURKEY-HUNT

• • •

dropped like a plummet. Shooting *chicalocki* was too easy, he decided; they presented so fair a mark that it was unfair to pull on them.

George was an impetuous hunter. Ken could not keep near him, nor coax nor command him to stay near. He would wander off by himself. That was one mark in his favor; at least he had no fear. Pepe hung close to Ken and Hal, with his dark eyes roving everywhere. Ken climbed out on one side of the swale, George on the other. Catching his whistle, Ken turned to look after him. He waved, and, pointing ahead, began to stoop and slip along from bush to bush. Presently a flock of Muscovy ducks rose before him, sailed a few rods, and alighted. Then from right under his feet labored up great gray birds. Wild geese! Ken recognized them as George's gun went *bang!* One tumbled over, the others wheeled toward the river. Ken started down into the swale to cross to where George was, when Pepe touched his arm.

"Turkeys!" he whispered.

That changed Ken's mind. Pepe pointed into the low bushes ahead and slowly led Ken forward. He heard a peculiar low thumping. Trails led everywhere, and here and there were open patches covered with a scant growth of grass. Across one of these flashed a bronze streak, then another and another.

"Shoot! Shoot!" said Pepe, tensely.

Those bronze streaks were running turkeys! The thumpings were made by their rapidly moving feet!

"Don't they flush—fly?" Ken queried of Pepe.

"No—no—shoot!" exclaimed he, as another streak of brown crossed an open spot. Ken hurriedly unbreached

129

• • •

his gun and changed the light shells for others loaded with heavy shot. He reached the edge of a bare spot across which a turkey ran with incredible swiftness. He did not get the gun in line with it at all. Then two more broke out of the bushes. Run! They were as swift as flying quail. Ken took two snap-shots, and missed both times. If anyone had told him that he would miss a running turkey at fifty feet, he would have been insulted. But he did not loosen a feather. Loading again, he yelled for George.

"Hey, George—turkeys!"

He whooped, and started across on the run.

"Gee!" said Hal. "Ken, I couldn't do any worse shooting than you. Let me take a few pegs."

Ken handed over the heavy gun and fell back a little, giving Hal the lead. They walked on, peering closely into the bushes. Suddenly a beautiful big gobbler ran out of a thicket, and then stopped to stretch out his long neck and look.

"Shoot—hurry!" whispered Ken. "What a chance!"

"That's a tame turkey," said Hal.

"Tame! Why, you tenderfoot! He's as wild as wild. Can't you see that?"

Ken's excitement and Pepe's intense eagerness all at once seemed communicated to Hal. He hauled up the gun, fingered the triggers awkwardly, then shot both barrels. He tore a tremendous hole in the brush some few feet to one side of the turkey. Then the great bird ran swiftly out of sight.

"Didn't want to kill him sitting, anyhow," said Hal, handing the gun back to Ken.

"We want to eat some turkey, don't we? Well, we'd

● ● ●

better take any chance. These birds are game, Hal, and don't you forget that!"

"What's all the shooting?" panted George, as he joined the march.

Just then there was a roar in the bushes, and a brown blur rose and whizzed ahead like a huge bullet. That turkey had flushed. Ken watched him fly till he went down out of sight into a distant swale.

"Pretty nifty flier, eh?" said George. "He was too quick for me."

"Great!" replied Ken.

There was another roar, and a huge bronze cannon-ball sped straight ahead. Ken shot both barrels, then George shot one, all clean misses. Ken watched this turkey fly, and saw him clearer. He had to admit that the wild turkey of the Tamaulipas jungle had a swifter and more beautiful flight than his favorite bird, the ruffled grouse.

"Walk faster," said George. "They'll flush better. I don't see how I'm to hit one. This goose I'm carrying weighs about a ton."

The hunters hurried along, crashing through the bushes. They saw turkey after turkey. *Bang!* went George's gun.

Then a beautiful sight made Ken cry out and forget to shoot. Six turkeys darted across an open patch—how swiftly they ran!—then rose in a bunch. The roar they made, the wonderfully rapid action of their powerful wings, and then the size of them, their wildness and no-ble gameness made them the royal game for Ken.

At the next threshing in the bushes his gun was lev-eled; he covered the whistling bronze thing that shot up.

● ● ●

The turkey went down with a crash. Pepe yelled, and as he ran forward the air all about him was full of fine bronze feathers. Ken hurried forward to see his bird. Its strength and symmetry, and especially the beautiful shades of bronze, captivated his eye.

"Come on, boys—this is the greatest game I ever hunted," he called.

Again Pepe yelled, and this time he pointed. From where Ken stood he could not see anything except low, green bushes. In great excitement George threw up his gun and shot. Ken heard a squealing.

"Javelin! Javelin!" yelled Pepe, in piercing alarm.

George jerked a rifle from him and began to shoot. Hal pumped his .22 into the bushes. The trampling of hard little hoofs and a cloud of dust warned Ken where the *javelin* were. Suddenly Pepe broke and fled for the river.

"Hyar, Pepe, fetch back my rifle," shouted Ken, angrily.

Pepe ran all the faster.

George turned and dashed away yelling: "Wild pigs! Wild pigs!"

"Look out, Ken! Run! Run!" added Hal, and he likewise took to his heels.

It looked as if there was nothing else for Ken to do but to make tracks from that vicinity. Never before had he run from a danger which he had not seen; but the flight of the boys was irresistibly contagious, and this, coupled with the many stories he had heard of the *javelin*, made Ken execute a spring that would have been a record but for the hampering weight of gun and turkey. He vowed he would hold on to both, pigs or no

132

● ● ●

pigs; nevertheless, he listened as he ran and nervously looked back often. It may have been excited imagination that the dust-cloud appeared to be traveling in his wake. Fortunately, the distance to the river did not exceed a short quarter of a mile. Hot, winded, and thoroughly disgusted with himself, Ken halted on the bank. Pepe was already in the boat, and George was scrambling aboard.

"A fine—chase—you've given—me," Ken panted. "There's nothing—after us."

"Don't you fool yourself," returned George, quickly. "I saw those pigs, and, like the ass I am, I blazed away at one with my shotgun."

"Did he run at you? That's what I want to know," demanded Ken.

George said he was not certain about that, but declared there always was danger if a wounded *javelin* squealed. Pepe had little to say; he refused to go back after the deer left in the trail. So they rowed across the shoal, and on the way passed within a rod of a big crocodile.

"Look at that fellow," cried George. "Wish I had my rifle loaded. He's fifteen feet long."

"Oh, no, George, he's not more than ten feet," said Ken.

"You don't see his tail. He's a whopper. Pepe told me there was one in this pool. We'll get him, all right."

They reached camp tired out, and all a little ruffled in temper, which certainly was not eased by the discovery that they were covered with ticks. Following the cue of his companions, Ken hurriedly stripped off his clothes and hung them where they could singe over the camp-fire. There were broad red bands of *pinilius* round both ankles, and reddish patches on the skin of his arms. Here and there were black spots about the size of his little fingernail, and these were *garrapatoes*. He picked these off one by one, rather surprised to find them come off so easily. Suddenly he jumped straight up with a pain as fierce as if it had been a puncture from a red-hot wire.

Pepe grinned, and George cried:

"Aha! that was a garrapato bite, that was! You just wait!"

George had a hundred or more of the big black ticks upon him, and he was remorselessly popping them with his cigarette. Some of them were biting him, too, judging from the way he flinched. Pepe had attracted to himself a million or more of the *pinilius*, but very few of the larger pests. He generously came to Ken's assistance. Ken was trying to pull off the *garrapato* that had bitten a hole in him. Pepe said it had embedded its head, and if pulled would come apart, leaving the head buried in the flesh, which would cause inflammation. Pepe held the glowing end of his cigarette close over the tick, and it began to squirm and pull out its head. When it was free of the flesh Pepe suddenly touched it with the cigarette, and it exploded with a pop. A difficult question was: Which hurt Ken the most, the burn from the cigarette or the bite of the tick? Pepe scraped off as many *pinilius* as would come, and then rubbed Ken with *canya*, the native alcohol. If this was not some kind of vitriol, Ken missed his guess. It smarted so keenly he thought his skin was peeling off. Presently, however, the smarting subsided, and so did the ticks.

A TURKEY-HUNT

• • •

Hal, who by far was the most sensitive one in regard to the crawling and biting of the jungle pests, had been remarkably fortunate in escaping them. So he made good use of his opportunity to poke fun at the others, particularly Ken.

George snapped out: "Just wait, Hollering Hal!"

"Don't you call me that!" said Hal, belligerently.

Ken eyed his brother in silence, but with a dark, meaning glance. It had occurred to Ken that here in this jungle was the only place in the world where he could hope to pay off old scores on Hal. And plots began to form in his mind.

They lounged about camp, resting in the shade during the hot midday hours. For supper they had a superfluity of meat, the waste of which Ken deplored, and he assuaged his conscience by deciding to have a taste of each kind. The wild turkey he found the most toothsome, delicious meat it had ever been his pleasure to eat. What struck him at once was the flavor, and he could not understand it until Pepe explained that the jungle turkey lived upon a red pepper. So the Tamaulipas wild turkey turned out to be doubly the finest game he had ever shot.

All afternoon the big crocodile sunned himself on the surface of the shoal.

Ken wanted a crocodile skin, and this was a chance to get one; but he thought it was well to wait, and kept the boys from wasting ammunition.

Before sundown Pepe went across the river and fetched the deer carcass down to the sand-bar, where the jaguar trail led to the water.

At twilight Ken stationed the boys at the lower end of the island, ambushed behind stones. He placed George

135

● ● ●

and Pepe some rods below his own position. They had George's .32 rifle and the 16-gauge loaded with a solid ball. Ken put Hal, with the double-barreled shotgun, also loaded with ball, some little distance above. And Ken, armed with his automatic, hid just opposite the deer trails.

"Be careful where you shoot," Ken warned repeatedly. "Be cool—think quick—and aim."

Ken settled down for a long wait, some fifty yards from the deer carcass. A wonderful procession of wild fowl winged swift flight over his head. They flew very low. It was strange to note the difference in the sounds of their flying. The cranes and herons softly swished the air, the teal and canvasbacks whirred by, and the great Muscovies whizzed like bullets.

When the first deer came down to drink it was almost dark, and when they left the moon was up, though obscured by clouds. Faint sounds rose from the other side of the island. Ken listened until his ears ached, but he could hear nothing. Heavier clouds drifted over the moon. The deer carcass became indistinct, and then faded entirely, and the bar itself grew vague. He was about to give up watching for that night when he heard a faint rustling below. Following it came a grating or crunching of gravel.

Bright flares split the darkness—*crack! crack!* rang out George's rifle, then the heavy *boom! boom!* of the shotgun.

"There he is!" yelled George. "He's down—we got him—there's two! Look out!" *Boom! Boom!* roared the heavy shotgun from Hal's covert.

A TURKEY-HUNT

• • •

"George missed him! I got him!" yelled Hal. "No, there he goes—Ken! Ken!"

Ken caught the flash of a long gray body in the hazy gloom of the bar and took a quick shot at it. The steel-jacketed bullet scattered the gravel and then hummed over the bank. The gray body moved fast up the bank. Ken could just see it. He turned loose the little automatic and made the welkin ring.

14

A Fight with a Jaguar

●

When the echoes of the shots died away the stillness
seemed all the deeper. No rustle in the brush or scuffle
on the sand gave evidence of a wounded or dying jaguar. George and Hal and Pepe declared that there were
two tigers and that they had hit one. Ken walked out
upon the stones till he could see the opposite bar, but
was not rewarded by a sight of dead game. Thereupon
they returned to camp, somewhat discouraged at their ill
luck, but planning another nightwatch.

In the morning George complained that he did not
feel well. Ken told him he had been eating too much
fresh meat and he had better be careful. Then Ken set
off alone, crossed the river, and found that the deer carcass was gone. In the sand near where it had lain were
plenty of cat tracks, but none of the big jaguar. Upon
closer scrutiny he found the cat tracks to be those of a

● ● ●

panther. He had half dragged, half carried the carcass up one of the steep trails, but from that point there was no further trace.

Ken struck out across the flat, intending to go as far as the jungle. Turtle-doves fluttered before him in numberless flocks. Far to one side he saw Muscovy ducks rising, sailing a few rods, then alighting. This occurred several times before he understood what it meant. There was probably a large flock feeding on the flat, and the ones in the rear were continually flying to get ahead of those to the fore.

Several turkeys ran through the bushes before Ken, but as he was carrying a rifle he paid little heed to them. He kept a keen lookout for *javelin*. Two or three times he was tempted to turn off the trail into little bamboo hollows; this, however, owing to a repugnance to ticks, he did not do. Finally, as he neared the high moss-decked wall of the jungle, he came upon a runway leading through the bottom of a deep swale, and here he found tiger tracks.

Farther down the swale, under a great cluster of bamboo, he saw the scattered bones of several deer. Ken was sure that in this spot the lord of the jungle had feasted more than once. It was an open hollow, with the ground bare under the bamboos. The runway led on into dense, leafy jungle. Ken planned to bait that lair with a deer carcass and watch it during the late afternoon.

First, it was necessary to get the deer. This might prove bothersome, for Ken's hands and wrists were already sprinkled with *pinilius*, and he certainly did not want to stay very long in the brush. Ken imagined he felt an itching all the time, and writhed inside his clothes.

"Say, blame you! Bite!" he exclaimed, resignedly, and stepped into the low bushes. He went up and out of the swale. Scarcely had he reached a level when he saw a troop of deer within easy range. Before they winded danger Ken shot, and the one he had singled out took a few bounds, then fell over sideways. The others ran off into the brush. Ken remembered that the old hunter on Penetier had told him how seldom a deer dropped at once. When he saw the work of the soft-nose .351 bullet, he no longer wondered at this deer falling almost in his tracks.

"If I ever hit a jaguar like that it will be all day with him," was Ken's comment.

There were two things about hunting the jaguar that Ken had been bidden to keep in mind—fierce aggressiveness and remarkable tenacity of life.

Ken dragged the deer down into the bamboo swale and skinned out a haunch. Next to wild turkey meat, he liked venison best. He was glad to have that as an excuse, for killing these tame tropical deer seemed like murder to Ken. He left the carcass in a favorable place and then hurried back to camp.

To Ken's relief, he managed to escape bringing any *garrapatoes* with him, but it took a half-hour to rid himself of the collection of *pinilius*.

"George, ask Pepe what's the difference between a garrapato and a pinilius," said Ken.

"The big tick is the little one's mother," replied Pepe.

"Gee! You fellows fuss a lot about ticks," said Hal, looking up from his task. He was building more pens to

• • •

accommodate the turtles, snakes, snails, mice, and young birds that he had captured during the morning.

Pepe said there were few ticks there in the uplands compared to the number down along the Panuco River. In the lowlands, where the cattle roamed, there were millions in every square rod. The under side of every leaf and blade of grass was red with ticks. The size of these pests depended on whether or not they got a chance to stick to a steer or any beast. They appeared to live indefinitely, but if they could not suck blood, they could not grow. The *pinilius* grew into a *garrapato*, and a *garrapato* bred a hundred thousand *pinilius* in her body. Two singular things concerning these ticks were that they always crawled upward and that they vanished from the earth during the wet season.

Ken soaked his Duxbax hunting suit in kerosene in the hope that this method would enable him to spend a reasonable time hunting. Then, while the other boys fished and played around, he waited for the long, hot hours to pass. It was cool in the shade, but the sunlight resembled the heat of fire. At last five o'clock came, and Ken put on the damp suit. Soaked with the oil, it was heavier and hotter than sealskin, and before he got across the river he was nearly roasted. The evening wind sprang up, and the gusts were like blasts from a furnace. Ken's body was bathed in perspiration; it ran down his wrists, over his hands, and wet the gun. This cure for ticks—if it were one—was worse than their bites. When he reached the shade of the bamboo swale it was none too soon for him. He threw off the coat, noticing there were more ticks upon it than at any time before. The bottom of his trousers, too, had gathered an exceeding quantity. He brushed them off, muttering the while that he believed they liked kerosene, and looked as if they were drinking it. Ken found it easy, however, to brush them off the wet Duxbax, and soon composed himself to rest and watch.

The position chosen afforded Ken a clear view of the bare space under the bamboos and of the hollow where the runway disappeared in the jungle. The deer carcass, which lay as he had left it, was about a hundred feet from him. This seemed rather close, but he had to accept it, for if he had moved farther away he could not have commanded both points.

Ken sat with his back against a clump of bamboos, the little rifle across his knees and an extra clip of cartridges on the ground at his left. After taking that position he determined not to move a yard when the tiger came, and to kill him.

Ken went over in his mind the lessons he had learned hunting bear in Penetier Forest with old Hiram Bent and lassoing lions on the wild north rim of the Grand Cañon. Ken knew that the thing for a hunter to do, when his quarry was dangerous, was to make up his mind beforehand. Ken had twelve powerful shells that he could shoot in the half of twelve seconds. He would have been willing to face two jaguars.

The sun set and the wind died down. What a relief was the cooling shade! The little breeze that was left fortunately blew at right angles to the swale, so that there did not seem much danger of the tiger winding Ken down the jungle runway.

For long moments he was tense and alert. He listened

● ● ●

till he thought he had almost lost the sense of hearing. The jungle leaves were whispering; the insects were humming. He had expected to hear myriad birds and see processions of deer, and perhaps a drove of *javelin*. But if any living creatures ventured near him it was without his knowledge. The hour between sunset and twilight passed—a long wait; still he did not lose the feeling that something would happen. Ken's faculties of alertness tired, however, and needed distraction. So he took stock of the big clump of bamboos under which lay the deer carcass.

It was a remarkable growth, that gracefully drooping cluster of slender bamboo poles. He remembered how, as a youngster, not many years back, he had wondered where the fishing-poles came from. Here Ken counted one hundred and sixty-nine in a clump no larger than a barrel. They were yellow in color with black bands, and they rose straight for a few yards, then began to lean out, to bend slightly, at last to droop with their abundance of spiked leaves. Ken was getting down to a real, interested study of this species of jungle growth when a noise startled him.

He straightened out of his lounging position and looked around. The sound puzzled him. He could not place its direction or name what it was. The jungle seemed strangely quiet. He listened. After a moment of waiting he again heard the sound. Instantly Ken was as tense and vibrating as a violin string. The thing he had heard was from the lungs of some jungle beast. He was almost ready to pronounce it a cough. Warily he glanced around, craning his neck. Then a deep, hoarse growl made him whirl.

● ● ●

There stood a jaguar with head up and paw on the deer carcass. Ken imagined he felt perfectly cool, but he knew he was astounded. And even as he cautiously edged the rifle over his knee he took in the beautiful points of the jaguar. He was yellow, almost white, with black spots. He was short and stocky, with powerful stumpy bow-legs. But his head most amazed Ken. It was enormous. And the expression of his face was so singularly savage and wild that Ken seemed to realize instantly the difference between a mountain-lion and this fierce tropical brute.

The jaguar opened his jaws threateningly. He had an enormous stretch of jaw. His long, yellow fangs gleamed. He growled again.

Nor hurriedly, nor yet slowly, Ken fired.

He heard the bullet strike him as plainly as if he had hit him with a board. He saw dust fly from his hide. Ken expected to see the jaguar roll over. Instead of that he leaped straight up with a terrible roar. Something within Ken shook. He felt cold and sick.

When the jaguar came down, sprawled on all fours, Ken pulled the automatic again, and he saw the fur fly. Then the jaguar leaped forward with a strange, hoarse cry. Ken shot again, and knocked the beast flat. He tumbled and wrestled about, scattering the dust and brush. Three times more Ken fired, too hastily, and inflicted only slight wounds.

In reloading Ken tried to be deliberate in snapping in the second clip and pushing down the rod that threw the shell into the barrel. But his hands shook. His fingers were all thumbs, and he fumbled at the breech of the rifle.

A FIGHT WITH A JAGUAR

• • •

In that interval, if the jaguar could have kept his sense of direction, he would have reached Ken. But the beast zigzagged; he had lost his equilibrium; he was hard hit.

Then he leaped magnificently. He landed within twenty-five feet of Ken, and when he plunged down he rolled clear over. Ken shot him through and through. Yet he got up, wheezing blood, uttering a hoarse bellow, and made again at Ken.

Ken had been cold, sick. Now panic almost overpowered him. The rifle wobbled. The bamboo glade blurred in his sight. A terrible dizziness and numbness almost paralyzed him. He was weakening, sinking, when thought of life at stake lent him a momentary grim and desperate spirit.

Once while the jaguar was in the air Ken pulled, twice while he was down. Then the jaguar stood up pawing the air with great spread claws, coughing, bleeding, roaring. He was horrible.

Ken shot him straight between the widespread paws.

With twisted body, staggering, and blowing bloody froth all over Ken, the big tiger blindly lunged forward and crashed to earth.

Then began a furious wrestling. Ken imagined it was the death throes of the jaguar. Ken could not see him down among the leaves and vines; nevertheless, he shot into the commotion. The struggles ceased. Then a movement of the weeds showed Ken that the jaguar was creeping toward the jungle.

Ken fell rather than sat down. He found he was wringing wet with cold sweat. He was panting hard.

145

KEN WARD IN THE JUNGLE

● ● ●

"Say, but—that—was—awful!" he gasped. "What—was—wrong—with me?"

He began to reload the clips. They were difficult to load for even a calm person, and now, in the reaction, Ken was the farthest removed from calm. The jaguar crept steadily away, as Ken could tell by the swaying weeds and shaking vines.

"What—a hard-lived beast!" muttered Ken. "I—must have shot—him all to pieces. Yet he's getting away from me."

At last Ken's trembling fingers pushed some shells in the two clips, and once more he reloaded the rifle. Then he stood up, drew a deep, full breath, and made a strong effort at composure.

"I've shot at bear—and deer—and lions out West," said Ken. "But this was different. I'll never get over it."

How close that jaguar came to reaching Ken was proved by the blood coughed into his face. He recalled that he had felt the wind of one great sweeping paw.

Ken regained his courage and determination. He meant to have that beautiful spotted skin for his den. So he hurried along the runway and entered the jungle. Beyond the edge, where the bushes made a dense thicket, it was dry forest, with little green low down. The hollow gave place to a dry wash. He could not see the jaguar, but he could hear him dragging himself through the brush, cracking sticks, shaking saplings.

Presently Ken ran across a bloody trail and followed it. Every little while he would stop to listen. When the wounded jaguar was still, he waited until he started to move again. It was hard going. The brush was thick, and had to be broken and crawled under or through. As

146

A FIGHT WITH A JAGUAR

• • •

Ken had left his coat behind, his shirt was soon torn to rags. He peered ahead with sharp eyes, expecting every minute to come in sight of the poor, crippled beast. He wanted to put him out of agony. So he kept on doggedly for what must have been a long time.

The first premonition he had of carelessness was to note that the shadows were gathering in the jungle. It would soon be night. He must turn back while there was light enough to follow his back track out to the open. The second came as a hot pain in his arm, as keen as if he had jagged it with a thorn. Holding it out, he discovered to his dismay that it was spotted with *garrapatoes*.

15

The Vicious Garrapatoes

●

At once Ken turned back, and if he thought again of the jaguar, it was that he could come after him the next day or send Pepe. Another vicious bite, this time on his leg, confirmed his suspicions that many of the ticks had been on him long enough to get their heads in. Then he was bitten in several places.

Those bites were as hot as the touch of a live coal, yet they made Ken break out in dripping cold sweat. It was imperative that he get back to camp without losing a moment which could be saved. From a rapid walk he fell into a trot. He got off his back trail and had to hunt for it. Every time a tick bit he jumped as if stung. The worst of it was that he knew he was collecting more *garrapatoes* with almost every step. When he grasped a dead branch to push it out of the way he could feel the ticks cling to his hand. Then he would whip his arm in

● ● ●

the air, flinging some of them off to patter on the dry ground. Impossible as it was to run through the matted jungle, Ken almost accomplished it. When he got out into the open he did run, not even stopping for his coat, and he crossed the flat at top speed.

It was almost dark when Ken reached the riverbank and dashed down to frighten a herd of drinking deer. He waded the narrowest part of the shoal. Running up the island he burst into the bright circle of camp-fire. Pepe dropped a stew-pan and began to jabber. George dove for a gun.

"What's after you?" shouted Hal, in alarm.

Ken was so choked up and breathless that at first he could not speak. His fierce aspect and actions, as he tore off his sleeveless and ragged shirt and threw it into the fire, added to the boys' fright.

"Good Lord! are you bug-house, Ken?" shrieked Hal.

"Bug-house! Yes!" roared Ken, swiftly undressing. "Look at me!"

In the bright glare he showed his arms black with *garrapatoes* and a sprinkling of black dots over the rest of his body.

"Is that all?" demanded Hal, in real or simulated scorn. "Gee, but you're a brave hunter. I thought not less than six tigers were after you."

"I'd rather have six tigers after me," yelled Ken. "You little freckle-faced red-head!"

It was seldom indeed that Ken called his brother that name. Hal was proof against any epithets except that one relating to his freckles and his hair. But just now Ken felt that he was being eaten alive. He was in an agony, and he lost his temper. And therefore he laid himself open to Hal's scathing humor.

"Never mind the kid," said Ken to Pepe and George. "Hurry now, and get busy with these devils on me."

It was well for Ken that he had a native like Pepe with him. For Pepe knew just what to do. First he dashed a bucket of cold water over Ken. How welcome that was!

"Pepe says for you to point out the ticks that're biting the hardest," said George.

In spite of his pain Ken stared in mute surprise.

"Pepe wants you to point out the ticks that are digging in the deepest," explained George. "Get a move on, now."

"What!" roared Ken, glaring at Pepe and George. He thought even the native might be having fun with him. And for Ken this was not a funny time.

But Pepe was in dead earnest.

"Say, it's impossible to tell *where* I'm being bitten most! It's all over!" protested Ken.

Still he discovered that by absolute concentration on the pain he was enduring he was able to locate the severest points. And that showed him the soundness of Pepe's advice.

"Here—this one—here—there. . . . Oh! here," began Ken, indicating certain ticks.

"Not so fast, now," interrupted the imperturbable George, as he and Pepe set to work upon Ken.

Then the red-hot cigarette tips scorched Ken's skin. Ken kept pointing and accompanying his directions with wild gestures and exclamations.

THE VICIOUS GARRAPATOES

●　●　●

"Here. . . . Oo-oo! Here. . . . Wow! Here. . . . Ouch!—
that one stung! Here. . . . *Augh!* Say, can't you hurry?
Here! . . . Oh! that one was in a mile! Here. . . . *Hold
on!* You're burning a hole in me! . . . George, you're
having fun out of this. Pepe gets two to your one."

"He's been popping ticks all his life," was George's
reasonable protest.

"Hurry!" cried Ken, in desperation. "George, if you
monkey round—fool over this job—I'll—I'll punch you
good."

All this trying time Hal Ward sat on a log and
watched the proceedings with great interest and humor.
Sometimes he smiled, at others he laughed, and yet
again he burst out into uproarious mirth.

"George, he wouldn't punch anybody," said Hal. "I
tell you he's all in. He hasn't any nerve left. It's a
chance of your life. You'll never get another. He's
been bossing you around. Pay him up. Make him hol-
ler. Why, what's a few little ticks? Wouldn't phase me!
But Ken Ward's such a delicate, fine-skinned, sensitive, girly kind of a boy! He's too nice to be bitten by
bugs. Oh dear, yes, yes!. . . Ken, why don't you show
courage?"

Ken shook his fist at Hal.

"All right," said Ken, grimly. "Have all the fun you
can. Because I'll get even with you."

Hal relapsed into silence, and Ken began to believe
he had intimidated his brother. But he soon realized
how foolish it was to suppose such a thing. Hal had
only been working his fertile brain.

"George, here's a little verse for the occasion," said
Hal.

KEN WARD IN THE JUNGLE

• • •

"There was a brave hunter named Ken,
And he loved to get skins for his den,
Not afraid was he of tigers or pigs,
Or snakes or cats or any such things,
But one day in the jungle he left his clothes,
And came hollering back with garrapatoes."

"Gre-at-t-t!" sputtered Ken. "Oh, brother mine, we're a long way from home. I'll make you crawl."

Pepe smoked and wore out three cigarettes, and George two, before they had popped all the biting ticks. Then Ken was still covered with them. Pepe bathed him in *canya*, which was like a bath of fire, and soon removed them all. Ken felt flayed alive, peeled of his skin, and sprinkled with fiery sparks. When he lay down he was as weak as a sick cat. Pepe said the *canya* would very soon take the sting away, but it was some time before Ken was resting easily.

It would not have been fair to ask Ken just then whether the prize for which he worked was worth his present gain. *Garrapatoes* may not seem important to one who simply reads about them, but such pests are a formidable feature of tropical life.

However, Ken presently felt that he was himself again.

Then he put his mind to the serious problem of his notebook and the plotting of the island. As far as his trip was concerned, Cypress Island was an important point. When he had completed his map down to the island, he went on to his notes. He believed that what he had found out from his knowledge of forestry was really worth something. He had seen a gradual increase in

THE VICIOUS GARRAPATOES

● ● ●

the size and number of trees as he had proceeded down the river, a difference in the density and color of the jungle, a flattening out of the mountain range, and a gradual change from rocky to clayey soil. And on the whole his notebook began to assume such a character that he was beginning to feel willing to submit it to his uncle.

16

Field Work of a Naturalist

•

That night Ken talked natural history to the boys and read extracts from a small copy of Sclater he had brought with him.

They were all particularly interested in the cat tribe.

The forefeet of all cats have five toes, the hindfeet only four. Their claws are curved and sharp, and, except in the case of one species of leopard, can be retracted in their sheaths. The claws of the great cat species are kept sharp by pulling them down through the bark of trees. All cats walk on their toes. And the stealthy walk is due to hairy pads or cushions. The claws of a cat do not show in its track as do those of a dog. The tongues of all cats are furnished with large papillae. They are like files, and are used to lick bones and clean their fur. Their long whiskers are delicate organs of perception to aid them in finding their way on their night quests. The

FIELD WORK OF A NATURALIST

• • •

eyes of all cats are large and full, and can be altered by contraction or expansion of the iris, according to the amount of light they receive. The usual color is gray or tawny with dark spots or stripes. The uniform tawny color of the lion and the panther is perhaps an acquired color, probably from the habit of these animals of living in desert countries. It is likely that in primitive times cats were all spotted or striped.

Naturally, the boys were most interested in the jaguar, which is the largest of the cat tribe in the New World. The jaguar ranges from northern Mexico to northern Patagonia. Its spots are larger than those of the leopard. Its ground color is a rich tan or yellow, sometimes almost gold. Large specimens have been known to be nearly seven feet from nose to end of tail.

The jaguar is an expert climber and swimmer. Humboldt says that where the South American forests are subject to floods the jaguar sometimes takes to tree life, living on monkeys. All naturalists agree on the ferocious nature of jaguars and on the loudness and frequency of their cries. There is no record of their attacking human beings without provocation. Their favorite haunts are the banks of jungle rivers, and they often prey upon fish and turtles.

The attack of a jaguar is terrible. It leaps on the back and breaks the neck of its prey. In some places there are well-known scratching trees where jaguars sharpen their claws. The bark is worn smooth in front from contact with the breasts of the animals as they stand up, and there is a deep groove on each side. When new scars appear on these trees it is known that jaguars are in the vicinity. The cry of the jaguar is loud, deep, hoarse,

• • •

something like *pu, pu, pu*. There is much enmity between the panther, or mountain-lion, and the jaguar, and it is very strange that generally the jaguar fears the lion, although he is larger and more powerful.

Pepe had interesting things to say about jaguars, or *tigres*, as he called them. But Ken, of course, could not tell how much Pepe said was truth and how much just native talk. At any rate, Pepe told of one Mexican who had a blind and deaf jaguar that he had tamed. Ken knew that naturalists claimed the jaguar could not be tamed, but in this instance Ken was inclined to believe Pepe. This blind jaguar was enormous in size, terrible of aspect, and had been trained to trail anything his master set him to. And Tigre, as he was called, never slept or stopped till he had killed the thing he was trailing. As he was blind and deaf, his power of scent had been abnormally developed.

Pepe told of a fight between a huge crocodile and a jaguar in which both were killed. He said jaguars stalked natives and had absolutely no fear. He knew natives who said that jaguars had made off with children and eaten them. Lastly, Pepe told of an incident that had happened in Tampico the year before. There was a ship at dock below Tampico, just on the outskirts where the jungle began, and one day at noon two big jaguars leaped on the deck. They frightened the crew out of their wits. George verified this story, and added that the jaguars had been chased by dogs, had boarded the ship, where they climbed into the rigging, and stayed there till they were shot.

"Well," said Ken, thoughtfully, "from my experience I believe a jaguar would do anything."

FIELD WORK OF A NATURALIST

• • •

The following day promised to be a busy one for Hal, without any time for tricks. George went hunting before breakfast—in fact, before the others were up—and just as the boys were sitting down to eat he appeared on the nearer bank and yelled for Pepe. It developed that for once George had bagged game.

He had a black squirrel, a small striped wildcat, a peccary, a three-foot crocodile, and a duck of rare plumage.

After breakfast Hal straightway got busy, and his skill and knowledge earned praise from George and Pepe. They volunteered to help, which offer Hal gratefully accepted. He had brought along a folding canvas tank, forceps, knives, scissors, several packages of preservatives, and tin boxes in which to pack small skins.

His first task was to mix a salt solution in the canvas tank. This was for immersing skins. Then he made a paste of salt and alum, and after that a mixture of two-thirds glycerin and one-third water and carbolic acid, which was to preserve small skins and to keep them soft.

And as he worked he gave George directions on how to proceed with the wildcat and squirrel skins.

"Skin carefully and tack up the pelts fur side down. Scrape off all the fat and oil, but don't scrape through. Tomorrow when the skins are dry soak them in cold water till soft. Then take them out and squeeze dry. I'll make a solution of three quarts water, one-half pint salt, and one ounce oil of vitriol. Put the skins in that for half an hour. Squeeze dry again, and hang in the shade. That'll tan the skins, and the moths will never hurt them."

KEN WARD IN THE JUNGLE

• • •

When Hal came to take up the duck he was sorry that some of the beautiful plumage had been stained.

"I want only a few water-fowl," he said. "And particularly one of the big Muscovies. And you must keep the feathers from getting soiled."

It was interesting to watch Hal handle that specimen. First he took full measurements. Then, separating the feathers along the breast, he made an incision with a sharp knife, beginning high up on the breastbone and ending at the tail. He exercised care so as not to cut through the abdomen. Raising the skin carefully along the cut as far as the muscles of the leg, he pushed out the knee joint and cut it off. Then he loosened the skin from the legs and the back, and bent the tail down to cut through the tail joint. Next he removed the skin from the body and cut off the wings at the shoulder joint. Then he proceeded down the neck, being careful not to pull or stretch the skin. Extreme care was necessary in cutting round the eyes. Then, when he had loosened the skin from the skull, he severed the head and cleaned out the skull. He coated all with the paste, filled the skull with cotton, and then immersed everything in the glycerin bath.

The skinning of the crocodile was an easy matter compared with that of the duck. Hal made an incision at the throat, cut along the middle of the abdomen all the way to the tip of the tail, and then cut the skin away all round the carcass. Then he set George and Pepe to scraping the skin, after which he immersed it in the tank.

About that time Ken, who was lazily fishing in the

158

shade of the cypresses, caught one of the blue-tailed fish. Hal was delighted. He had made a failure of the other specimen of this unknown fish. This one was larger and exquisitely marked, being dark gold on the back, white along the belly, and its tail had a faint bluish tinge. Hal promptly killed the fish, and then made a dive for his suitcase. He produced several sheets of stiff cardboard and a small box of water-colors and brushes. He laid the fish down on a piece of paper and outlined its exact size. Then, placing it carefully in an upright position on a box, he began to paint it in the actual colors of the moment. Ken laughed and teased him. George also was inclined to be amused. But Pepe was amazed and delighted. Hal worked on unmindful of his audience, and, though he did not paint a very artistic picture, he reproduced the vivid colors of the fish before they faded.

His next move was to cover the fish with strips of thin cloth, which adhered to the scales and kept them from being damaged. Then he cut along the middle line of the belly, divided the pelvic arch where the ventral fins joined, cut through the spines, and severed the fins from the bones. Then he skinned down to the tail, up to the back, and cut through the caudal processes. The vertebral column he severed at the base of the skull. He cleaned and scraped the entire inside of the skin, and then put it to soak.

"Hal, you're much more likely to make good with Uncle Jim than I am," said Ken. "You've really got skill, and you know what to do. Now, my job is different. So far I've done fairly well with my map of the

• • •

river. But as soon as we get on level ground I'll be stumped."

"We'll cover a hundred miles before we get to low land," replied Hal, cheerily. "That's enough, even if we do get lost for the rest of the way. You'll win that trip abroad, Ken, never fear, and little Willie is going to be with you."

17

A Mixed-up
Tiger-hunt

•

Next morning Hal arose bright as a lark, but silent,
mysterious, and with far-seeing eyes. It made Ken
groan in spirit to look at the boy. Yes, indeed, they were
far from home, and the person did not live on the earth
who could play a trick on Hal Ward and escape ven-
geance.

After breakfast Hal went off with a long-handled
landing-net, obviously to capture birds or fish or mice
or something.

George said he did not feel very well, and he looked
grouchy. He growled around camp in a way that might
have nettled Ken, but Ken, having had ten hours of un-
disturbed sleep, could not have found fault with anybody.

"Garrapato George, come out of it. Cheer up," said
Ken. "Why don't you take Pinilius Pepe as gun-bearer

and go out to shoot something? You haven't used up *much* ammunition yet."

Ken's sarcasm was not lost upon George.

"Well, if I do go, I'll not come running back to camp without some game."

"My son," replied Ken, genially, "if you should happen to meet a jaguar you'd—you'd just let out one squawk and then never touch even the high places of the jungle. You'd take that crazy .32 rifle for a golf-stick."

"Would I?" returned George. "All right."

Ken watched George awhile that morning. The lad performed a lot of weird things around camp. Then he bounced bullets off the water in a vain effort to locate the basking crocodile. Then he tried his hand at fishing once more. He could get more bites than any fisherman Ken ever saw, but he could not catch anything.

By and by the heat made Ken drowsy, and, stretching himself in the shade, he thought of a scheme to rid the camp of the noisy George.

"Say, George, take my hammerless and get Pepe to row you up along the shady bank of the river," suggested Ken. "Go sneaking along and you'll have some sport."

George was delighted with that idea. He had often cast longing eyes at the hammerless gun. Pepe, too, looked exceedingly pleased. They got in the boat and were in the act of starting when George jumped ashore. He reached for his .32 and threw the lever down to see if there was a shell in the chamber. Then he proceeded to fill his pockets with ammunition.

A MIXED-UP TIGER-HUNT

• • •

"Might need a rifle," he said. "You can't tell what you're going to see in this unholy jungle."

Whereupon he went aboard again and Pepe rowed leisurely upstream.

"Be careful, boys," Ken called, and composed himself for a nap. He promptly fell asleep. How long he slept he had no idea, and when he awoke he lay with languor, not knowing at the moment what had awakened him. Presently he heard a shout, then a rifle shot. Sitting up, he saw the boat some two hundred yards above, drifting along about the edge of the shade. Pepe was in it alone. He appeared to be excited, for Ken observed him lay down an oar and pick up a gun, and then reverse the performance. Also he was jabbering to George, who evidently was out on the bank, but invisible to Ken.

"Hey, Pepe!" Ken yelled. "What're you doing?"

Strange to note, Pepe did not rely or even turn.

"Now where in the deuce is George?" Ken said, impatiently.

The hollow crack of George's .32 was a reply to the question. Ken heard the singing of a bullet. Suddenly, *spou!* it twanged on a branch not twenty feet over his head, and then went whining away. He heard it tick a few leaves or twigs. There was not any languor in the alacrity with which Ken put the big cypress tree between him and upstream. Then he ventured to peep forth.

"Look out where you're slinging lead!" he yelled. He doubted not that George had treed a black squirrel or was pegging away at parrots. Yet Pepe's motions appeared to carry a good deal of feeling, too much, he

● ● ●

thought presently, for small game. So Ken began to wake up thoroughly. He lost sight of Pepe behind the low branch of a tree that leaned some fifty yards above the island. Then he caught sight of him again. He was poling with an oar, evidently trying to go up or down— Ken could not tell which.

Spang! Spang! George's .32 spoke twice more, and the bullets both struck in the middle of the stream and ricocheted into the far bank with little thuds.

Something prompted Ken to reach for his automatic, snap the clip in tight, and push in the safety. At the same time he muttered George's words: "You can never tell what's coming off in this unholy jungle."

Then, peeping out from behind the cypress, Ken watched the boat drift downstream. Pepe had stopped poling and was looking closely into the thick grass and vines of the bank. Ken heard his voice, but could not tell what he said. He watched keenly for some sight of George. The moments passed, the boat drifted, and Ken began to think there was nothing unusual afoot. In this interval Pepe drifted within seventy-five yards of camp. Again Ken called to ask him what George was stalking, and this time Pepe yelled; but Ken did not know what he said. Hard upon this came George's sharp voice:

"Look out, there, on the island. Get behind something. I've got him between the river and the flat. He's in this strip of shore brush. There!"

Spang! Spang! Spang! Bullets hummed and whistled

all about the island. Ken was afraid to peep out with even one eye. He began to fancy that George was playing Indian.

"Fine, Georgie! You're doing great!" he shouted. "You couldn't come any closer to me if you were aiming at me. What is it?"

Then a crashing of brush and a flash of yellow low down along the bank changed the aspect of the situation.

"Panther! Or jaguar!" Ken ejaculated, in amaze. In a second he was tight-muscled, cold, and clear-witted. At that instant he saw George's white shirt about the top of the brush.

"Go back! Get out in the open!" Ken ordered. "Do you hear me?"

"Where is he?" shouted George, paying not the slightest attention to Ken. Ken jumped from behind the tree, and, running to the head of the island, he knelt low near the water with rifle ready.

"Tigre! Tigre! Tigre!" screamed Pepe, waving his arms, then pointing.

George crashed into the brush. Ken saw the leaves move, then a long yellow shape. With the quickness of thought and the aim of the wing-shot, Ken fired. From the brush rose a strange wild scream. George aimed at a shaking mass of grass and vines, but, before he could fire, a long, lean, ugly beast leaped straight out from the bank to drop into the water with a heavy splash.

Like a man half scared to death Pepe waved Ken's double-barreled gun. Then a yellow head emerged from

165

● ● ●

the water. It was in line with the boat. Ken dared not shoot.

"Kill him, George," yelled Ken. "Tell Pepe to kill him."

George seemed unaccountably silent. But Ken had no time to look for him, for his eyes were riveted on Pepe. The native did not know how to hold a gun properly, let alone aim it. He had, however, sense enough to try. He got the stock under his chin, and, pointing the gun, he evidently tried to fire. But the hammerless did not go off. Then Pepe fumbled at the safety-catch, which he evidently remembered seeing Ken use.

The jaguar, swimming with difficulty, perhaps badly wounded, made right for the boat. Pepe was standing on the seat. Awkwardly he aimed.

Boom! He had pulled both triggers. The recoil knocked him backward. The hammerless fell in the boat, and Pepe's broad back hit the water; his bare, muscular legs clung to the gunwale, and slipped loose.

He had missed the jaguar, for it kept on toward the boat. Still Ken dared not shoot.

"George, what on earth is the matter with you?" shouted Ken.

Then Ken saw him standing in the brush on the bank, fussing over the crazy .32. Of course at the critical moment something had gone wrong with the old rifle.

Pepe's head bobbed up just on the other side of the boat. The jaguar was scarcely twenty feet distant and now in line with both boat and man. At that instant a heavy swirl in the water toward the middle of the

● ● ●

river drew Ken's attention. He saw the big crocodile, and the great creature did not seem at all lazy at that moment.

George began to scream in Spanish. Ken felt his hair stiffen and his face blanch. Pepe, who had been solely occupied with the jaguar, caught George's meaning and turned to see the peril in his rear.

He bawled his familiar appeal to the saints. Then he grasped the gunwale of the boat just as it swung against the branches of the low-leaning tree. He vaulted rather than climbed aboard.

Ken forgot that Pepe could understand little English, and he yelled: "Grab an oar, Pepe. Keep the jaguar in the water. Don't let him in the boat."

But Pepe, even if he had understood, had a better idea. Nimble, he ran over the boat and grasped the branches of the tree just as the jaguar flopped paws and head over the stern gunwale.

Ken had only a fleeting instant to get a bead on that yellow body, and before he could be sure of an aim the branch weighted with Pepe sank down to hide both boat and jaguar. The chill of fear for Pepe changed to hot rage at this new difficulty.

Then George began to shoot.

Spang!

Ken heard the bullet hit the boat.

"George—wait!" shouted Ken. "Don't shoot holes in the boat. You'll sink it."

Spang! Spang! Spang! Spang!

That was as much as George cared about such a possibility. He stood on the bank and worked the lever of

● ● ●

his .32 with wild haste. Ken plainly heard the spat of the bullets, and the sound was that of lead in contact with wood. So he knew George was not hitting the jaguar.

"You'll ruin the boat!" roared Ken.

Pepe had worked up from the lower end of the branch, and as soon as he straddled it and hunched himself nearer shore the foliage rose out of the water, exposing the boat. George kept on shooting till his magazine was empty. Ken's position was too low for him to see the jaguar.

Then the boat swung loose from the branch and, drifting down, gradually approached the shore.

"Pull yourself together, George," called Ken. "Keep cool. Make sure of your aim. We've got him now."

"He's mine! He's mine! He's mine! Don't you dare shoot!" howled George. "I got him!"

"All right. But steady up, can't you? Hit him once, anyway."

Apparently without aim George fired. Then, jerking the lever, he fired again. The boat drifted into overhanging vines. Once more Ken saw a yellow and black object, then a trembling trail of leaves.

"He's coming out below you. Look out," yelled Ken.

George disappeared. Ken saw no sign of the jaguar and heard no shot or shout from George. Pepe dropped from his branch to the bank and caught the boat. Ken called, and while Pepe rowed over to the island, he got into some clothes fit to hunt in. Then they hurried back across the channel to the bank.

A MIXED-UP TIGER-HUNT

● ● ●

Ken found the trail of the jaguar, followed it up to the edge of the brush, and lost it in the weedy flat. George came out of a patch of bamboos. He looked white and shaky and wild with disappointment.

"Oh, I had a dandy shot as he came out, but the blamed gun jammed again. Come on, we'll get him. He's all shot up. I bet I hit him ten times. He won't get away."

Ken finally got George back to camp. The boat was half full of water, making it necessary to pull it out on the bank and turn it over. There were ten bullet-holes in it.

"George, you hit the boat, anyway," Ken said. "Now we've a job on our hands."

Hal came puffing into camp. He was red of face, and the sweat stood out on his forehead. He had a small animal of some kind in a sack, and his legs were wet to his knees.

"What was—all the—pegging about?" he asked, breathlessly. "I expected to find camp surrounded by Indians."

"Kid, it's been pretty hot round here for a little. George and Pepe rounded up a tiger. Tell us about it, George," said Ken.

So while Ken began to whittle pegs to pound into the bullet-holes, George wiped his flushed, sweaty face and talked.

"We were up there a piece, round the bend. I saw a black squirrel and went ashore to get him. But I couldn't find him, and in kicking round in the brush I came into a kind of trail or runway. Then I ran plumb

169

into that darned jaguar. I was so scared I couldn't remember my gun. But the cat turned and ran. It was
lucky he didn't make at me. When I saw him run I got
back my courage. I called for Pepe to row downstream
and keep a lookout. Then I got into the flat. I must have
come down a good ways before I saw him. I shot, and
he dodged back into the brush again. I fired into the
moving bushes where he was. And pretty soon I ventured to get in on the bank, where I had a better chance.
I guess it was about that time that I heard you yell.
Then it all happened. You hit him! Didn't you hear him
scream? What a jump he made! If it hadn't been so terrible when your hammerless kicked Pepe overboard, I
would have died laughing. Then I was paralyzed when
the jaguar swam for the boat. He was hurt, for the water
was bloody. Things came off quick, I tell you. Like a
monkey Pepe scrambled into the tree. When I got my
gun loaded the jaguar was crouched down in the bottom
of the boat watching Pepe. Then I began to shoot. I
can't realize he got away from us. What was the reason
you didn't knock him?"

"Well, you see, George, there were two good rea-
sons," Ken replied. "The first was that at that time I
was busy dodging bullets from your rifle. And the second was that you threatened my life if I killed your jaguar."

"Did I get as nutty as that? But it was pretty warm
there for a little. . . . Say, was he a big one? My eyes
were so hazy I didn't see him clear."

"He wasn't big, not half as big as the one I lost yesterday. Yours was a long, wiry beast, like a panther, and
mean-looking."

A MIXED-UP TIGER-HUNT

● ● ●

Pepe sat on the bank, and while he nursed his bruises he smoked. Once he made a speech that was untranslatable, but Hal gave it an interpretation which was probably near correct.

"That's right, Pepe. Pretty punk tiger-hunters—mucho punk!"

18

Watching a Runway

●

"I'll tell you what, fellows," said Hal. "I know where we *can* get a tiger."

"We'll get one in the neck if we don't watch out," replied George.

Ken thought that Hal looked very frank and earnest, and honest and eager, but there was never any telling about him.

"Where?" he asked, skeptically.

"Down along the river. You know I've been setting traps all along. There's a flat sand-bar for a good piece down. I came to a little gully full of big tracks, big as my two hands. And fresh!"

"Honest Injun, kid?" queried Ken.

"Hope to die if I'm lyin'," replied Hal. "I want to see somebody kill a tiger. Now let's go down there in the boat and wait for one to come to drink. There's a big log with driftwood lodged on it. We can hide behind that."

"Great idea, Hal," said Ken. "We'd be pretty safe in the boat. I want to say that tigers have sort of got on my nerves. I ought to go over in the jungle to look for the one I crippled. He's dead by now. But the longer I put it off the harder it is to go. I'll back out yet. . . . Come, we'll have an early dinner. Then watch for Hal's tiger."

The sun had just set, and the hot breeze began to swirl up the river when Ken slid the boat into the water. He was pleased to find that it did not leak.

"We'll take only two guns," said Ken, "my .351 and the hammerless, with some ball-cartridges. We want to be quiet tonight, and if you fellows take your guns you'll be pegging at ducks and things. That won't do."

Pepe sat at the oars with instructions to row easily. George and Hal occupied the stern-seats, and Ken took his place in the bow, with both guns at hand.

The hot wind roared in the cypresses, and the river whipped up little waves with white crests. Long streamers of gray moss waved out over the water and branches tossed and swayed. The blow did not last for many minutes. Trees and river once more grew quiet. And suddenly the heat was gone.

As Pepe rowed on down the river, Cypress Island began to disappear round a bend, and presently was out of sight. Ducks were already in flight. They flew low over the boat, so low that Ken could almost have reached them with the barrel of his gun. The river here widened. It was full of huge snags. A high, wooded bluff shadowed the western shore. On the left, towering

173

cypresses, all laced together in dense vine and moss webs, leaned out.

Under Hal's direction Pepe rowed to a pile of driftwood, and here the boat was moored. The gully mentioned by Hal was some sixty yards distant. It opened like the mouth of a cave. Beyond the cypresses thick, intertwining bamboos covered it.

"I wish we'd gone in to see the tracks," said Ken. "But I'll take your word, Hal."

"Oh, they're there, all right."

"I don't doubt it. Looks great to me! That's a runway, Hal. . . . Now, boys, get a comfortable seat, and settle down to wait. Don't talk. Just listen and watch. Remember, soon we'll be out of the jungle, back home. So make hay while the sun shines. Watch and listen! Whoever sees or hears anything first is the best man."

For once the boys were as obedient as lambs. But then, Ken thought, the surroundings were so beautiful and wild and silent that any boys would have been watchful.

There was absolutely no sound but the intermittent whir of wings. The water-fowl flew by in companies— ducks, cranes, herons, snipe, and the great Muscovies. Ken never would have tired of that procession. It passed all too soon, and then only an occasional water-fowl swept swiftly by, as if belated.

Slowly the wide river-lane shaded. But it was still daylight, and the bank and the runway were clearly distinguishable. There was a moment—Ken could not tell just how he knew—when the jungle awakened. It was not only the faint hum of insects; it was a sense that life stirred with the coming of twilight.

WATCHING A RUNWAY

• • •

Pepe was the first to earn honors at the listening game. He held up a warning forefinger. Then he pointed under the bluff. Ken saw a doe stepping out of a fringe of willows.

"Don't move—don't make a noise," whispered Ken.

The doe shot up long ears and watched the boat. Then a little fawn trotted out and splashed in the water. Both deer drank, then seemed in no hurry to leave the river.

Next moment Hal heard something downstream and George saw something upstream. Pepe again whispered. As for Ken, he saw little dark shapes moving out of the shadow of the runway. He heard a faint trampling of hard little hoofs. But if these animals were *javelin*—of which he was sure—they did not come out into the open runway. Ken tried to catch Pepe's attention without making a noise; however, Pepe was absorbed in his side of the river. Ken then forgot he had companions. All along the shores were faint splashings and rustlings and crackings.

A loud, trampling roar rose in the runway and seemed to move backward toward the jungle, diminishing in violence.

"Pigs running—something scared 'em," said George.

"S-s-s-sh!" whispered Ken.

All the sounds ceased. The jungle seemed to sleep in deep silence.

Ken's eyes were glued to the light patch of sand bank where it merged in the dark of the runway. Then Ken heard a sound—what, he could not have told. But it made his heart beat fast.

There came a few pattering thuds, soft as velvet; and

175

• • •

a shadow, paler than the dark background, moved out of the runway.

With that a huge jaguar loped into the open. He did not look round. He took a long, easy bound down to the water and began to lap.

Either Pepe or George jerked so violently as to make the boat lurch. They seemed to be stifling.

"Oh, Ken, don't miss!" whispered Hal.

Ken had the automatic over the log and in line. His teeth were shut tight, and he was cold and steady. He meant not to hurry.

The jaguar was a heavy, squat, muscular figure, not graceful and beautiful like the one Ken had crippled. Suddenly he raised his head and looked about. He had caught a scent.

It was then that Ken lowered the rifle till the sight covered the beast—lower yet to his huge paws, then still lower to the edge of the water. Ken meant to shoot low enough this time. Holding the rifle there, and holding it with all his strength, he pressed the trigger once—twice. The two shots rang out almost simultaneously. Ken expected to see this jaguar leap, but the beast crumpled up and sank in his tracks.

Then the boys yelled, and Ken echoed them. Pepe was wildly excited, and began to fumble with the oars.

"Wait! Wait, I tell you!" ordered Ken.

"Oh, Ken, you pegged him!" cried Hal. "He doesn't move. Let's go ashore. What did I tell you? It took me to find the tiger."

Ken watched with sharp eyes and held his rifle ready, but the huddled form on the sand never so much as twitched.

"I guess I plugged him," said Ken, with unconscious pride.

Pepe rowed the boat ashore, and when near the sandbar he reached out with an oar to touch the jaguar. There was no doubt about his being dead. The boys leaped ashore and straightened out the beast. He was huge, dirty, spotted, bloody, and fiercely savage even in death. Ken's bullets had torn through the chest, making fearful wounds. Pepe jabbered, and the boys all talked at once. When it came to lifting the jaguar into the boat they had no slight task. The short, thick-set body was very heavy. But at last they loaded it in the bow, and Pepe rowed back to the island. It was still a harder task to get the jaguar up the high bank. Pepe kindled a fire so they would have plenty of light, and then they set to work at the skinning.

What with enthusiasm over the stalk, and talk of the success of the trip, and compliments to Ken's shooting, and care of the skinning, the boys were three hours at the job. Ken, remembering Hiram Bent's teachings, skinned out the great claws himself. They salted the pelt and nailed it up on the big cypress.

"You'd never have got one but for me," said Hal. "That's how I pay you for the tricks you've played me!"

"By George, Hal, it's a noble revenge!" cried Ken, who, in the warmth and glow of happiness of the time, quite believed his brother.

Pepe went to bed first. George turned in next. Ken took a last look at the great pelt stretched on the cypress, and then he sought his blankets. Hal, however,

● ● ●

remained up. Ken heard him pounding stakes in the ground.

"Hal, what're you doing?"

"I'm settin' my trot-lines," replied Hal, cheerfully.

"Well, come to bed."

"Keep your shirt on, Ken, old boy. I'll be along presently."

Ken fell asleep. He did not have peaceful slumbers. He had been too excited to rest well. He would wake up out of a nightmare, then go to sleep again. He seemed to wake suddenly out of one of these black spells, and he was conscious of pain. Something tugged at his leg.

"What the dickens!" he said, and raised on his elbow. Hal was asleep between George and Pepe, who were snoring.

Just then Ken felt a violent jerk. The blankets flew up at his feet, and his left leg went out across his brother's body. There was a string—a rope—something fast round his ankle, and it was pulling hard. It hurt.

"Jiminy!" shouted Ken, reaching for his foot. But before he could reach it another tug, more violent, pulled his leg straight out. Ken began to slide.

"What on earth?" yelled Ken. "Say! Something's got me!"

The yells and Ken's rude exertions aroused the boys. And they were frightened. Ken got an arm around Hal and the other around George and held on for dear life. He was more frightened than they. Pepe leaped up, jabbering, and, tripping, he fell all in a heap.

"Oh! my leg!" howled Ken. "It's being pulled off. Say, I can't be dreaming!"

Most assuredly Ken was wide awake. The moonlight

showed his bare leg sticking out and round his ankle a heavy trot-line. It was stretched tight. It ran down over the bank. And out there in the river a tremendous fish or a crocodile was surging about, making the water roar.

Pepe was trying to loosen the line or break it. George, who was always stupid when first aroused, probably imagined he was being mauled by a jaguar, for he loudly bellowed. Ken had a stranglehold on Hal.

"Oh! *Oh! Oh-h-h!*" bawled Ken. Not only was he scared out of a year's growth, he was in terrible pain. Then his cries grew unintelligible. He was being dragged out of the tent. Still he clung desperately to the howling George and the fighting Hal.

All at once something snapped. The tension relaxed. Ken fell back upon Hal.

"Git off me, will you?" shouted Hal. "Are you c-c-cr-azy?"

But Hal's voice had not the usual note when he was angry or impatient. He was laughing so he could not speak naturally.

"Uh-huh!" said Ken, and sat up. "I guess here was where I got it. Is my leg broken? What came off?"

Pepe was staggering about on the bank, going through strange motions. He had the line in his hands, and at the other end was a monster of some kind threshing about in the water. It was moonlight and Ken could see plainly. Around the ankle that felt broken was a twisted loop of trot-line. Hal had baited a hook and slipped the end of the trot-line over Ken's foot. During the night the crocodile or an enormous fish had taken the bait. Then Ken had nearly been hauled off the island.

KEN WARD IN THE JUNGLE

• • •

Pepe was doing battle with the hooked thing, whatever it was, and Ken was about to go to his assistance when again the line broke.

"Great! Hal, you have a nice disposition," exclaimed Ken. "You have a wonderful affection for your brother. You care a lot about his legs or his life. Idiot! Can't you play a safe trick? If I hadn't grabbed you and George, I'd have been pulled into the river. Eaten up, maybe! And my ankle is sprained. It won't be any good for a week. You are a bright boy!"

And in spite of his laughter Hal began to look ashamed.

19

Adventures with Crocodiles

●

The rest of that night Ken had more dreams, and they were not pleasant. He awoke from one in a cold fright.

It must have been late, for the moon was low. His ankle pained and throbbed, and to that he attributed his nightmare. He was falling asleep again when the clink of tin pans made him sit up with a start. Some animal was prowling about camp. He peered into the moonlit shadows, but could make out no unfamiliar object. Still he was not satisfied, so he awoke Pepe.

Certainly it was not Ken's intention to let Pepe get out ahead; nevertheless, he was lame and slow, and before he started Pepe rolled out of the tent.

"Santa Maria!" shrieked Pepe.

Ken fumbled under his pillow for a gun. Hal raised up so quickly that he bumped Ken's head, making him

● ● ●

see a million stars. George rolled over, nearly knocking down the tent.

From outside came a sliddery, rustling noise, then another yell that was deadened by a sounding splash. Ken leaped out with his gun, George at his elbow. Pepe stood just back of the tent, his arms upraised, and he appeared stunned. The water near the bank was boiling and bubbling; waves were dashing on the shore and ripples spreading in a circle.

George shouted in Spanish.

"Crocodile!" cried Ken.

"Si, si, Señor," replied Pepe. Then he said that when he stepped out of the tent the crocodile was right in camp, not ten feet from where the boys lay. Pepe also said that these brutes were man-eaters and that he had better watch for the rest of the night. Ken thought him, like all the natives, inclined to exaggerate; however, he made no objection to Pepe's holding watch over the crocodile.

"What'd I tell you?" growled George. "Why didn't you let me shoot him? Let's go back to bed."

In the morning when Ken got up he viewed his body with great curiosity. The ticks and the cigarette burns had left him a beautifully tattooed specimen of aborigine. His body, especially his arms, bore hundreds of little reddish scars—bites and burns together. There was not, however, any itching or irritation, for which he had to thank Pepe's skill and the *canya*.

George did not get up when Ken called him. Thinking his sleep might have been broken, Ken let him alone a while longer, but when breakfast was smoking

ADVENTURES WITH CROCODILES

• • •

he gave him a prod. George rolled over, looking haggard and glum.

"I'm sick," he said.

Ken's cheerfulness left him, for he knew what sickness or injury did to a camping trip. George complained of aching bones, headache, and cramps and showed a tongue with a yellow coating. Ken said he had eaten too much fresh meat, but Pepe, after looking George over, called it a name that sounded like *calentura*.

"What's that?" Ken inquired.

"Tropic fever," replied George. "I've had it before."

For a while he was a very sick boy. Ken had a little medicine case, and from it he administered what he thought was best, and George grew easier presently. Then Ken sat down to deliberate on the situation.

Whatever way he viewed it, he always came back to the same thing—they must get out of the jungle; and as they could not go back, they must go on down the river. That was a bad enough proposition without being hampered by a sick boy. It was then Ken had a subtle change of feeling; a shade of gloom seemed to pervade his spirit.

By nine o'clock they were packed, and, turning into the shady channel, soon were out in the sunlight saying good-by to Cypress Island. At the moment Ken did not feel sorry to go, yet he knew that that feeling would come by and by and that Cypress Island would take its place in his memory as one more haunting, calling wild place.

They turned a curve to run under a rocky bluff from which came a muffled roar of rapids. A long, projecting point of rock extended across the river, allowing the

183

water to rush through only at a narrow mill-race channel close to the shore. It was an obstacle to get around. There was no possibility of lifting the boat over the bridge of rock, and the alternative was shooting the channel. Ken got out upon the rocks, only to find that drifting the boat round the sharp point was out of the question, owing to a dangerously swift current. Ken tried the depth of the water—about four feet. Then he dragged the boat back a little distance and stepped into the river.

"Look! Look!" cried Pepe, pointing to the bank.

About ten yards away was a bare shelf of mud glistening with water and showing the deep tracks of a crocodile. It was a slide, and manifestly had just been vacated. The crocodile tracks resembled the imprints of a giant's hand.

"Come out!" yelled George, and Pepe jabbered to his saints.

"We've got to go down this river," Ken replied, and he kept on wading till he got the boat in the current. He was frightened, of course, but he kept on despite that. The boat lurched into the channel, stern first, and he leaped up on the bow. It shot down with the speed of a toboggan, and the boat whirled before he could scramble to the oars. What was worse, an overhanging tree with dead snags left scarce room to pass beneath. Ken ducked to prevent being swept overboard, and one of the snags that brushed and scraped him ran under his belt and lifted him into the air. He grasped at the first thing he could lay hands on, which happened to be a box, but he could not hold to it because the boat threatened to go on, leaving him kicking in midair and hold-

• • •

ing up a box of potatoes. Ken clutched a gunwale, only to see the water swell dangerously over the edge. In angry helplessness he loosened his hold. Then the snag broke, just in the nick of time, for in a second more the boat would have been swept away. Ken fell across the bow, held on, and soon drifted from under the threshing branches, and seized the oars.

Pepe and George and Hal walked round the ledge and, even when they reached Ken, had not stopped laughing.

"Boys, it wasn't funny," declared Ken, soberly.

"I said it was coming to us," replied George.

There were rapids below, and Ken went at them with stern eyes and set lips. It was the look of men who face obstacles in getting out of the wilderness. More than one high wave circled spitefully round Pepe's broad shoulders.

They came to a fall where the river dropped a few feet straight down. Ken sent the boys below. Hal and George made a detour. But Pepe jumped off the ledge into shallow water.

"Ah-h!" yelled Pepe.

Ken was becoming accustomed to Pepe's wild yell, but there was a note in this which sent a shiver over him. Before looking, Ken snatched his rifle from the boat.

Pepe appeared to be sailing out into the pool. But his feet were not moving.

Ken had only an instant, but in that he saw under Pepe a long, yellow, swimming shape, leaving a wake in the water. Pepe had jumped upon the back of a crocodile. He seemed paralyzed, or else he was wisely trusting himself there rather than in the water. Ken was too shocked to offer advice. Indeed, he would not have known how to meet this situation.

Suddenly Pepe leaped for a dry stone, and the energy of his leap carried him into the river beyond. Like a flash he was out again, spouting water.

Ken turned loose the automatic on the crocodile and shot a magazine of shells. The crocodile made a tre- mendous surge, churning up a slimy foam, then van- ished in a pool.

"Guess this'll be crocodile day," said Ken, changing the clip in his rifle. "I'll bet I made a hole in that one. Boys, look out below."

Ken shoved the boat over the ledge in line with Pepe, and it floated to him, while Ken picked his way round the rocky shore. The boys piled aboard again. The day began to get hot. Ken cautioned the boys to avoid wad- ing, if possible, and to be extremely careful where they stepped. Pepe pointed now and then to huge bubbles breaking on the surface of the water and said they were made by crocodiles.

From then on Ken's hands were full. He struck swift water, where rapid after rapid, fall on fall, took the boat downhill at a rate to afford him satisfaction. The current had a five or six mile speed, and, as Ken had no por- tages to make and the corrugated rapids of big waves gave him speed, he made by far the best time of the voyage.

The hot hours passed—cool for the boys because they were always wet. The sun sank behind a hill. The wind ceased to whip the streamers of moss. At last, in

● ● ●

a gathering twilight, Ken halted at a wide, flat rock to make camp.

"Forty miles today if we made an inch!" exclaimed Ken.

The boys said more.

They built a fire, cooked supper, and then, weary and silent, Hal and George and Pepe rolled into their blankets. But Ken doggedly worked an hour at his map and notes. That hard forty miles meant a long way toward the success of his trip.

Next morning the mists had not lifted from the river when they shoved off, determined to beat the record of yesterday. Difficulties beset them from the start—the highest waterfall of the trip, a leak in the boat, deep, short rapids, narrows with choppy waves, and a whirl-pool where they turned round and round, unable to row out. Nor did they get free till Pepe lassoed a snag and pulled them out.

About noon they came to another narrow chute brawling down into a deep, foamy pool. Again Ken sent the boys around, and he backed the boat into the chute; and just as the current caught it he leaped aboard. He was either tired or careless, for he drifted too close to a half-submerged rock, and, try as he might, at the last moment he could not avoid a collision.

As the stern went hard on the rock Ken expected to break something, but was surprised at the soft thud with which he struck. It flashed into his mind that the rock was moss-covered.

Quick as the thought there came a rumble under the boat, the stern heaved up, there was a great sheet-like splash, and then a blow that splintered the gunwale.

● ● ●

Then the boat shunted off, affording the astounded Ken a good view of a very angry crocodile. He had been sleeping on the rock.

The boys were yelling and crowding down to the shore where Ken was drifting in. Pepe waded in to catch the boat.

"What was it hit you, Ken?" asked Hal.

"Mucho malo," cried Pepe.

"The boat's half full of water—the gunwale's all split!" ejaculated George.

"Only an accident of river travel," replied Ken, with mock nonchalance. "Say, Garrapato, *when*, about *when* is it coming to me?"

"Well, if he didn't get slammed by a crocodile!" continued George.

They unloaded, turned out the water, broke up a box to use for repairs, and mended the damaged gunwale—work that lost more than a good hour. Once again under way, Ken made some interesting observations. The river ceased to stand on end in places; crocodiles slipped off every muddy promontory, and wide trails ridged the steep clay banks.

"Cattle trails, Pepe says," said George. "Wild cattle roam all through the jungle along the Panuco."

It was a well-known fact that the rancheros of Tamaulipas State had no idea how many cattle they owned. Ken was so eager to see if Pepe had been correct that he went ashore to find the trails were, indeed, those of cattle.

"Then, Pepe, we must be somewhere near the Panuco River," he said.

"Quien sabe?" rejoined he, quietly.

ADVENTURES WITH CROCODILES

● ● ●

When they rounded the curve they came upon a herd of cattle that clattered up the bank, raising a cloud of dust.

"Wilder than deer!" Ken exclaimed.

From that point conditions along the river changed. The banks were no longer green; the beautiful cypresses gave place to other trees, as huge, as moss-wound, but more rugged and of gaunt outline; the flowers and vines and shady nooks disappeared. Everywhere wide-horned steers and cows plunged up the banks. Everywhere buzzards rose from gruesome feasts. The shore was lined with dead cattle, and the stench of putrefying flesh was almost unbearable. They passed cattle mired in the mud, being slowly tortured to death by flies and hunger; they passed cattle that had slipped off steep banks and could not get back and were bellowing dismally; and also strangely acting cattle that Pepe said had gone crazy from ticks in their ears. Ken would have put these miserable beasts out of their misery had not George restrained him with a few words about Mexican law.

A sense of sickness came to Ken, and though he drove the feeling from him, it continually returned. George and Hal lay flat on the canvas, shaded with a couple of palm leaves; Pepe rowed on and on, growing more and more serious and quiet. His quick, responsive smile was wanting now.

By way of diversion, and also in the hope of securing a specimen, Ken began to shoot at the crocodiles. George came out of his lethargy and took up his rifle. He would have had to be ill indeed, to forswear any possible shooting; and, now that Ken had removed the bar, he forgot he had fever. Every hundred yards or so

they would come upon a crocodile measuring somewhere from about six feet upward, and occasionally
they would see a great yellow one, as large as a log.
Seldom did they get within good range of these huge
fellows, and shooting from a moving boat was not easy.
The smaller ones, however, allowed the boat to approach quite close. George bounced many a .32 bullet
off the bank, but he never hit a crocodile. Ken allowed
him to have the shots for the fun of it, and, besides, he
was watching for a big one.

"George, that rifle of yours is leaded. It doesn't shoot
where you aim."

When they got unusually close to a small crocodile
George verified Ken's statement by missing his game
some yards. He promptly threw the worn-out rifle overboard, an act that caused Pepe much concern.

Whereupon Ken proceeded to try his luck. Instructing
Pepe to row about in the middle of the stream, he kept
eye on one shore while George watched the other. He
shot half a dozen small crocodiles, but they slipped off
the bank before Pepe could get ashore. This did not appear to be the fault of the rifle, for some of the reptiles
were shot almost in two pieces. But Ken had yet to
learn more about the tenacity of life of these water-
brutes. Several held still long enough for Ken to shoot
them through, then with a plunge they went into the water, sinking at once in a bloody foam. He knew he had
shot them through, for he saw large holes in the mud
banks lined with bits of bloody skin and bone.

"There's one," said George, pointing. "Let's get
closer, so we can grab him. He's got a good piece to go
before he reaches the water."

ADVENTURES WITH CROCODILES

● ● ●

Pepe rowed slowly along, guiding the boat a little nearer the shore. At forty feet the crocodile raised up, standing on short legs, so that all but his tail was free of the ground. He opened his huge jaws either in astonishment or to intimidate them, and then Ken shot him straight down the throat. He flopped convulsively and started to slide and roll. When he reached the water he turned over on his back, with his feet sticking up, resembling a huge frog. Pepe rowed hard to the shore, just as the crocodile with one last convulsion rolled off into deeper water. Ken reached over, grasped his foot, and was drawing it up when a sight of cold, glassy eyes and open-fanged jaws made him let go. Then the crocodile sank in water where Pepe could not touch bottom with an oar.

"Let's get one if it takes a week," declared George. The lad might be sick, but there was nothing wrong with his spirit. "Look there!" he exclaimed. "Oh, I guess it's a log. Too big!"

They had been unable to tell the difference between a crocodile and a log of driftwood until it was too late. In this instance a long, dirty gray object lay upon a low bank. Despite its immense size, which certainly made the chances in favor of its being a log, Ken determined this time to be fooled on the right side. He had seen a dozen logs—as he thought—suddenly become animated and slip into the river.

"Hold steady, Pepe. I'll take a crack at that just for luck."

The distance was about a hundred yards, a fine range for the little rifle. Resting on his knee, he sighted low, under the gray object, and pulled the trigger twice.

● ● ●

There were two *spats* so close together as to be barely distinguishable. The log of driftwood leaped into life.

"Whoop!" shouted Hal.

"It's a crocodile!" yelled George. "You hit—you hit! Will you listen to that?"

"Row hard, Pepe—pull!"

He bent to the oars, and the boat flew shoreward.

The huge crocodile, opening yard-long jaws, snapped them shut with loud cracks. Then he beat the bank with his tail. It was as limber as a willow, but he seemed unable to move his central parts, his thick bulk, where Ken had sent the two mushroom bullets. *Whack! Whack! Whack!* The sodden blows jarred pieces from the clay bank above him. Each blow was powerful enough to have staved in the planking of a ship. All at once he lunged upward and, falling over backward, slid down his runway into a few inches of water, where he stuck.

"Go in above him, Pepe," Ken shouted. "Here— Heavens! What a monster!"

Deliberately, at scarce twenty feet, Ken shot the remaining four shells into the crocodile. The bullets tore through his horny hide, and blood and muddy water spouted up. George and Pepe and Hal yelled, and Ken kept time with them. The terrible lashing tail swung back and forth almost too swiftly for the eye to catch. A deluge of mud and water descended upon the boys, bespattering, blinding them and weighing down the boat. They jumped out upon the bank to escape it. They ran to and fro in aimless excitement. Ken still clutched the rifle, but he had no shells for it. George was absurd enough to fling a stone into the blood-tinged cloud of

• • •

muddy froth and spray that hid the threshing leviathan. Presently the commotion subsided enough for them to see the great crocodile lying half on his back, with belly all torn and bloody and huge claw-like hands pawing the air. He was edging, slipping off into deeper water.

"He'll get away—he'll get away!" cried Hal. "What'll we do?"

Ken racked his brains.

"Pepe, get your lasso—rope him—rope him! Hurry! He's slipping!" yelled George.

Pepe snatched up his lariat, and, without waiting to coil it, cast the loop. He caught one of the flippers and hauled tight on it just as the crocodile slipped out of sight off the muddy ledge. The others ran to the boat, and, grasping hold of the lasso with Pepe, squared away and began to pull. Plain it was that the crocodile was not coming up so easily. They could not budge him.

"Hang on, boys!" Ken shouted. "It's a tug-of-war."

The lasso was suddenly jerked out with a kind of twang. Crash! went Pepe and Hal into the bottom of the boat. Ken went sprawling into the mud, and George, who had the last hold, went to his knees, but valiantly clung to the slipping rope. Bounding up, Ken grasped it from him and wound it round the sharp nose of the bowsprit.

"Get in—hustle!" he called, falling aboard. "You're always saying it's coming to us. Here's where!"

George had hardly got into the boat when the crocodile pulled it off shore, and away it went, sailing downstream.

"Whoop! All aboard for Panuco!" yelled Hal.

• • •

"Now, Pepe, you don't need to row any more—we've a water-horse," Ken added.

But Pepe did not enter into the spirit of the occasion. He kept calling on the saints and crying, "Mucho malo." George and Ken and Hal, however, were hilarious. They had not yet had experience enough to know crocodiles.

Faster and faster they went. The water began to surge away from the bow and leave a gurgling wake behind the stern. Soon the boat reached the middle of the river where the water was deepest, and the lasso went almost straight down.

Ken felt the stern of the boat gradually lifted, and then, in alarm, he saw the front end sinking in the water. The crocodile was hauling the bow under.

"Pepe—your machete—cut the lasso!" he ordered, sharply. George had to repeat the order.

Wildly Pepe searched under the seat and along the gunwales. He could not find the *machete*.

"Cut the rope!" Ken thundered. "Use a knife, the ax—anything—only cut it—and cut it quick!"

Pepe could find nothing. Knife in hand, Ken leaped over his head, sprawled headlong over the trunk, and slashed the taut lasso just as the water began to roar into the boat. The bow bobbed up as a cork that had been under. But the boat had shipped six inches of water.

"Row ashore, Pepe. Steady, there. Trim the boat, George."

They beached at a hard clay bank and rested a little before unloading to turn out the water.

"Grande!" observed Pepe.

• • •

"Yes, he was big," assented George.

"I wonder what's going to happen to us next," added Hal.

Ken Ward looked at these companions of his and he laughed outright. "Well, if you all don't take the cake for nerve!"

20

Treed by Wild Pigs

•

Pepe's long years of *mozo* work, rowing for tarpon fishermen, now stood the boys in good stead. All the hot hours of the day he bent steadily to the oars. Occasionally they came to rifts, but these were not difficult to pass, being mere swift, shallow channels over sandy bottom. The rocks and the rapids were things of the past.

George lay in a kind of stupor, and Hal lolled in his seat. Ken, however, kept alert, and as the afternoon wore on began to be annoyed at the scarcity of campsites.

The muddy margins of the river, the steep banks, and the tick-infested forests offered few places where it was possible to rest, to say nothing of sleep. Every turn in the widening river gave Ken hope, which resulted in disappointment. He found consolation, however, in the

196

● ● ●

fact that every turn and every hour put him so much farther on the way.

About five o'clock Ken had unexpected good luck in
the shape of a small sand-bar cut off from the mainland,
and therefore free of cattle tracks. It was clean and dry,
with a pile of driftwood at one end.

"Tumble out, boys," called Ken, as Pepe beached the
boat. "We'll pitch camp here."

Neither Hal nor George showed any alacrity. Ken
watched his brother; he feared to see some of the symp-
toms of George's sickness. Both lads, however, seemed
cheerful, though too tired to be of much use in the
pitching of camp.

Ken could not recover his former good spirits. There
was a sense of foreboding in his mind that all was not
well, that he must hurry, hurry. And although George
appeared to be holding his own, Hal healthy enough,
and Pepe's brooding quiet at least no worse, Ken could
not rid himself of gloom. If he had answered the question that knocked at his mind he would have admitted a
certainty of disaster. So he kept active, and when there
were no more tasks for that day he worked on his notebook, and then watched the flight of wild fowl.

The farther down the river the boys traveled the more
numerous were the herons and cranes and ducks. But
they saw no more of the beautiful *pato real*, as Pepe
called them, or the little russet-colored ducks, or the
dismal-voiced bitterns. On the other hand, wild geese
were common, and there were flocks and flocks of teal
and canvasbacks.

Pepe, as usual, cooked duck. And he had to eat it.
George had lost his appetite altogether. Hal had lost his

taste for meat, at least. And Ken made a frugal meal of rice.

"Boys," he said, "the less you eat from now on the better for you."

It took resolution to drink the cocoa, for Ken could not shut out the remembrance of the green water and the shoreline of dead and decaying cattle. Still, he was parched with thirst; he had to drink. That night he slept ten hours without turning over. Next morning he had to shake Pepe to rouse him.

Ken took turns at the oars with Pepe. It was not only that he fancied Pepe was weakening and in need of an occasional rest, but the fact that he wanted to be occupied, and especially to keep in good condition. They made thirty miles by four o'clock, and most of it against a breeze. Not in the whole distance did they pass a dozen places fit for a camp. Toward evening the river narrowed again, resembling somewhat the Santa Rosa of earlier acquaintance. The magnificent dark forests crowded high on the banks, always screened and curtained by gray moss, as if to keep their secrets.

The sun was just tipping with gold the mossy crests of a grove of giant ceibas, when the boys rounded a bend to come upon the first ledge of rocks for two days. A low, grassy promontory invited the eyes searching for camping-ground. This spot appeared ideal; it certainly was beautiful. The ledge jutted into the river almost to the opposite shore, forcing the water to rush through a rocky trough into a great foam-spotted pool below.

They could not pitch the tent, since the stony ground would not admit stakes, so they laid the canvas flat. Pepe went up the bank with his *machete* in search of

● ● ●

firewood. To Ken's utmost delight he found a little spring of sweet water trickling from the ledge, and by digging a hole was enabled to get a drink, the first one in more than a week.

A little later, as he was spreading the blankets, George called his attention to shouts up in the woods.

"Pepe's treed something," Ken said. "Take your gun and hunt him up."

Ken went on making a bed and busying himself about the camp, with little heed to George's departure. Presently, however, he was startled by unmistakable sounds of alarm. George and Pepe were yelling in unison, and, from the sound, appeared to be quite a distance away.

"What the deuce!" Ken ejaculated, snatching up his rifle. He snapped a clip in the magazine and dropped several loaded clips and a box of extra shells into his coat pocket. After his adventure with the jaguar he decided never again to find himself short of ammunition. Running up the sloping bank, he entered the forest, shouting for his companions. Answering cries came from in front and a little to the left. He could not make out what was said.

Save for drooping moss the forest was comparatively open, and at a hundred paces from the riverbank were glades covered with thickets and long grass and short palm trees. The ground sloped upward quite perceptibly.

"Hey, boys, where are you?" called Ken.

Pepe's shrill yells mingled with George's shouts. At first their meaning was unintelligible, but after calling twice Ken understood.

KEN WARD IN THE JUNGLE

● ● ●

"Javelin! Go back! Javelin! We're treed! Wild pigs! Santa Maria! Run for your life!"

This was certainly enlightening and rather embarrassing. Ken remembered the other time the boys had made him run, and he grew hot with anger.

"I'll be blessed if I'll run!" he said, in the pride of conceit and wounded vanity. Whereupon he began to climb the slope, stopping every few steps to listen and look. Ken wondered what had made Pepe go so far for firewood; still, there was nothing but green wood all about. Walking round a clump of seared and yellow palms that rustled in the breeze, Ken suddenly espied George's white shirt. He was in a scrubby sapling not fifteen feet from the ground. Then Ken espied Pepe, perched in the forks of a ceiba, high above the thickets and low shrubbery. Ken was scarcely more than a dozen rods from them down the gradual slope. Both saw him at once.

"Run, you Indian! Run!" bawled George, waving his hands.

George implored Ken to fly to save his precious life.

"What for? You fools! I don't see anything to run from," Ken shouted back. His temper had soured a little during the last few days.

"You'd better run, or you'll have to climb," replied George. "Wild pigs—a thousand of 'em!"

"Where?"

"Right under us. There! Oh, if they see you! Listen to this." He broke off a branch, trimmed it of leaves, and flung it down. Ken heard a low, trampling roar of many hard little feet, brushings in the thicket, and cracking of twigs. As close as he was, however, he

● ● ●

could not see a moving object. The dead grass and brush were several feet high, up to his waist in spots, and, though he changed position several times, no *javelin* did he see.

"You want to look out. Say, man, these are wild pigs—boars, I tell you! They'll kill you!" bellowed George.

"Are you going to stay up there all night?" Ken asked, sarcastically.

"We'll stay till they go away."

"All right, I'll scare them away," Ken replied, and, suiting action to word, he worked the automatic as fast as it would shoot, aiming into the thicket under George.

Of all the foolish things a nettled hunter ever did that was the worst. A roar answered the echoes of the rifle, and the roar rose from every side of the trees the victims were in. Nervously Ken clamped a fresh clip of shells into the rifle. Clouds of dust arose, and strange little squeals and grunts seemed to come from every quarter. Then the grass and bushes were suddenly torn apart by swift gray forms with glittering eyes. They were everywhere.

"Run! Run!" shrieked George, high above the tumult.

For a thrilling instant Ken stood his ground and fired at the bobbing gray backs. But every break made in the ranks by the powerful shells filled in a flash. Before that vicious charge he wavered, then ran as if pursued by demons.

The way was downhill. Ken tripped, fell, rolled over and over, then, still clutching the rifle, rose with a bound and fled. The *javelin* had gained. They were at his heels. He ran like a deer. Then, seeing a low branch,

KEN WARD IN THE JUNGLE

* * *

he leaped for it, grasped it with one hand, and, crooking an elbow round it, swung with the old giant swing.

Before Ken knew how it had happened he was astride a dangerously swaying branch directly over a troop of brownish-gray, sharp-snouted, fiendish-eyed little peccaries.

Some were young and sleek, others were old and rough, some had yellow teeth or tusks, and all pointed their sharp noses upward, as if expecting him to fall into their very mouths. Feeling safe, once more Ken loaded the rifle and began to kill the biggest, most vicious *javelin*. When he had killed twelve in twelve shots, he saw that shooting a few would be of no avail. There were hundreds, it seemed, and he had scarcely fifty shells left. Moreover, the rifle-barrel grew so hot that it burnt his hands. Hearing George's yell, he replied, somewhat to his disgust:

"I'm all right, George—only treed. How're you?"

"Pigs all gone—they chased you—Pepe thinks we can risk running."

"Don't take any chances," Ken yelled, in answer.

"Hi! Hi! What's wrong with you gazabos?" came Hal's yell from down the slope.

"Go back to the boat," shouted Ken.

"What for?"

"We're all treed by javelin—wild pigs."

"I've got to see that," was Hal's reply.

Ken called a sharp, angry order for Hal to keep away. But Hal did not obey. Ken heard him coming, and presently saw him enter one of the little glades. He had Ken's shotgun, and was peering cautiously about.

"Ken, where are you?"

TREED BY WILD PIGS

• • •

"Here! Didn't I tell you to keep away? The pigs heard you—some of them are edging out there. Look out! Run, kid, run!"

A troop of *javelin* flashed into the glade. Hal saw them and raised the shotgun.

Boom! He shot both barrels.

The shot tore through the brush all around Ken, but fortunately beneath him. Neither the noise nor the lead stopped the pugnacious little peccaries.

Hal dropped Ken's hammerless and fled.

"Run faster!" yelled George, who evidently enjoyed Hal's plight. "They'll get you! Run hard!"

The lad was running close to the record when he disappeared.

In trying to find a more comfortable posture, so he could apply himself to an interesting study of his captors, Ken made the startling discovery that the branch which upheld him was splitting from the tree trunk. His heart began to pound in his breast; then it went up into his throat. Every move he made—for he had started to edge toward the tree—widened the little white split.

"Boys, my branch is breaking!" he called, piercingly.

"Can't you get another?" returned George.

"No, I daren't move! Hurry, boys! If you don't scare these brutes off I'm a goner!"

Ken's eyes were riveted upon the gap where the branch was slowly separating from the tree trunk. He glanced about to see if he could not leap to another branch. There was nothing near that would hold him. In desperation he resolved to drop the rifle, cautiously get to his feet upon the branch, and with one spring try to reach the tree. When about to act upon this last chance he heard Pepe's shrill yell and a crashing in the brush. Then followed the unmistakable roar and crackling of fire. Pepe had fired the brush—no, he was making his way toward Ken, armed with a huge torch.

"Pepe, you'll fire the jungle!" cried Ken, forgetting what was at stake and that Pepe could not understand much English. But Ken had been in one forest fire and remembered it with horror.

The *javelin* stirred uneasily, and ran around under Ken, tumbling over one another.

When Pepe burst through the brush, holding before him long-stemmed palm leaves flaring in hissing flames, the whole pack of pigs bowled away into the forest at breakneck speed.

Ken leaped down, and the branch came with him. George came running up, his face white, his eyes big. Behind him rose a roar that Ken thought might be another drove of pigs till he saw smoke and flame.

"Boys, the jungle's on fire. Run for the river!"

In their hurry they miscalculated the location of camp and dashed out of the jungle over a steep bank, and they all had a tumble. It was necessary to wade to reach the rocky ledge.

Ken shook hands with Pepe.

"George, tell him that was a nervy thing to do. He saved my life, I do believe."

"You fellows did a lot of hollering," said Hal, from his perch in the boat.

"Say, young man, you've got to go back after my gun. Why didn't you do what I told you? Foolish to run into danger that way!" declared Ken, severely.

TREED BY WILD PIGS

• • •

"You don't suppose I was going to overlook a chance to see Ken Ward treed, do you?"

"Well, you saw him, and that was no joke. But I wish Pepe could have scared those pigs off without firing the jungle."

"Pepe says it'll give the ticks a good roasting," said George.

"We'll have roast pig, anyway," added Ken.

He kept watching the jungle back of the camp as if he expected it to blow up like a powder mine. But this Tamaulipas jungle was not Penetier Forest. A cloud of smoke rolled up; there was a frequent roaring of dry palms; but the green growths did not burn. It was not much of a forest fire, and Ken concluded that it would soon burn out.

So he took advantage of the waning daylight to spread out his map and plot in the day's travel. This time Hal watched him with a quiet attention that was both flattering and stimulating, and at the conclusion of the task he said:

"Well, Ken, we're having sport, but we're doing something more—something worthwhile."

21

The Leaping Tarpon

●

Just before dark, when the boys were at supper, a swarm of black mosquitoes swooped down upon camp.

Pepe could not have shown more fear at angry snakes, and he began to pile green wood and leaves on the fire to make a heavy smoke.

These mosquitoes were very large, black-bodied, with white-barred wings. Their bite was as painful as the sting of a bee. After threshing about until tired out the boys went to bed. But it was only to get up again, for the mosquitoes could bite through two thicknesses of blanket.

For a wonder everyone was quiet. Even George did not grumble. The only thing to do was to sit or stand in the smoke of the camp-fire. The boys wore their gloves

● ● ●

and wrapped blankets round their heads and shoulders. They crouched over the fire until tired of that position, then stood up till they could stand no longer. It was a wretched, sleepless night with the bloodthirsty mosquitoes humming about like a swarm of bees. They did not go away until dawn.

"That's what I get for losing the mosquito-netting," said Ken, wearily.

Breakfast was not a cheerful meal, despite the fact that the boys all tried to brace up.

George's condition showed Ken the necessity for renewed efforts to get out of the jungle. Pepe appeared heavy and slow, and, what was more alarming, he had lost his appetite. Hal was cross, but seemed to keep well. It was hard enough for Ken to persuade George and Pepe to take the bitter doses of quinine, and Hal positively refused.

"It makes me sick, I tell you," said Hal, impatiently.

"But Hal, you ought to be guided by my judgment now," replied Ken, gently.

"I don't care. I've had enough of bitter pills."

"I ask you—as a favor?" persisted Ken, quietly.

"No!"

"Well, then, I'll have to make you take them."

"Wha-at?" roared Hal.

"If necessary, I'll throw you down and pry open your mouth and get Pepe to stuff these pills down your throat. There!" went on Ken, and now he did not recognize his own voice.

Hal looked quickly at his brother, and was amazed and all at once shaken.

"Why, Ken—" he faltered.

"I ought to have made you take them before," interrupted Ken. "But I've been too easy. Now, Hal, listen— and you, too, George. I've made a bad mess of this trip. I got you into this jungle, and I ought to have taken better care of you, whether you would or not. George has fever. Pepe is getting it. I'm afraid you won't escape. You all *would* drink unboiled water."

"Ken, that's all right, but you can get fever from the bites of the ticks," said George.

"I dare say. But just the same you could have been careful about the water. Not only that—look how careless we have been. Think of the things that have happened! We've gotten almost wild on this trip. We don't realize. But wait till we get home. Then we'll hardly be able to believe we ever had these adventures. But our foolishness, our carelessness, *must* stop right here. If we can't profit by our lucky escapes yesterday—from that lassoed crocodile and the wild pigs—we are simply no good. I love fun and sport. But there's a limit. Hal, remember what old Hiram told you about being foolhardily brave. I think we have been wonderfully lucky. Now let's deserve our good luck. Let's not prove what that Tampico hotel man said. Let's show we are not just wild-goose-chasing boys. I put it to you straight. I think the real test is yet to come, and I want you to help me. No more tricks. No more drinking unboiled water. No more shooting except in self-defense. We must not eat any more meat. No more careless wandering up the banks. No chances. See? And fight the fever. Don't give up. Then when we get out of this awful jungle we can

THE LEAPING TARPON

● ● ●

look back at our adventures—and, better, we can be sure we've learned a lot. We shall have accomplished something, and that's learning. Now, how about it? Will you help me?"

"You can just bet your life," replied George, and he held out his hand.

"Ken, I'm with you," was Hal's quiet promise, and Ken knew from the way the lad spoke that he was in dead earnest. When it came to the last ditch Hal Ward was as true as steel. He took the raw, bitter quinine Ken offered and swallowed it without a grimace.

"Good!" exclaimed Ken. "Now, boys, let's pack. Hal, you let your menagerie go. There's no use keeping your pets any longer. George, you make yourself a bed on the trunk, and fix a palm leaf sun-shelter. Then lie down."

When the boat had been packed and all was in readiness for the start, George was sound asleep. They shoved off into the current. Pepe and Ken took turns at the oars, making five miles an hour.

As on the day before, they glided under the shadows of the great moss-twined cypresses, along the muddy banks where crocodiles basked in the sun and gaunt cattle came down to drink. Once the boat turned a bushy point to startle a large flock of wild turkeys, perhaps thirty-five in number. They had been resting in the cool sand along the river. Some ran up the bank, some half-dozen flew right over the boat, and most of them squatted down as if to evade detection. Thereafter turkeys and ducks and geese became so common as to be monotonous.

KEN WARD IN THE JUNGLE

• • •

About one o'clock Ken sighted a thatched bamboo and palm leaf hut on the bank.

"Oh, boys, look! look!" cried Ken, joyfully.

Hal was as pleased as Ken, and George roused out of his slumber. Pepe grinned and nodded his head.

Some naked little children ran like quail. A disheveled black head peeped out of a door, then swiftly vanished.

"Indians," said George.

"I don't care," replied Ken, "they're human beings— people. We're getting somewhere."

From there on the little bamboo huts were frequently sighted. And soon Ken saw a large one situated upon a high bluff. Ken was wondering if these natives would be hospitable.

Upon rounding the next bend the boys came unexpectedly upon a connecting river. It was twice as wide as the Santa Rosa and quite swift.

"Tamaulipas," said Pepe.

"Hooray! boys, this is the source of the Panuco, sure as you're born," cried Ken. "I told you we were getting somewhere."

He was overcome with the discovery. This meant success.

"Savalo! Savalo!" exclaimed Pepe, pointing.

"Tarpon! Tarpon! What do you think of that? Way up here! We must be a long distance from tide-water," said George.

Ken looked around over the broad pool below the junction of the two rivers. And here and there he saw swirls, and big splashes, and then the silver sides of rolling tarpon.

210

THE LEAPING TARPON

● ● ●

"Boys, seeing we've packed that can of preserved mullet all the way, and those thundering heavy tackles, let's try for tarpon," suggested Ken.

It was wonderful to see how the boys responded. Pepe was no longer slow and heavy. George forgot he was sick. Hal, who loved to fish better than to hunt, was as enthusiastic as on the first day.

"Ken, let me boss this job," said George, as he began to rig the tackles. "Pepe will row; you and Hal sit back here and troll. I'll make myself useful. Open the can. See, I hook the mullet just back of the head, letting the barb come out free. There! Now run out about forty feet of line. Steady the butt of the rod under your leg. Put your left hand above the reel. Hold the handle of the reel in your right, and hold it hard. The drag is in the handle. Now when a tarpon takes the bait, jerk with all your might. Their mouths are like iron, and it's hard to get a hook to stick."

Pepe rowed at a smooth, even stroke and made for the great curve of the pool where tarpon were breaking water.

"If they're on the feed, we'll have more sport than we've had yet," said George.

Ken was fascinated, and saw that Hal was going to have the best time of the trip. Also Ken was very curious to have a tarpon strike. He had no idea what it would be like. Presently, when the boat glided among the rolling fish and there was prospect of one striking at any moment, Ken could not subdue a mounting excitement.

"Steady now—be ready," warned George.

● ● ●

Suddenly Hal's line straightened. The lad yelled and jerked at the same instant. There came a roar of splitting waters, and a beautiful silver fish, longer than Hal himself, shot up into the air. The tarpon shook himself and dropped back into the water with a crash.

Hal was speechless. He wound in his line to find the bait gone.

"Threw the hook," said George, as he reached into the can for another bait. "He wasn't so big. You'll get used to losing 'em. There! try again."

Ken had felt several gentle tugs at his line, as if tarpon were rolling across it. And indeed he saw several fish swim right over where his line disappeared in the water. There were splashes all around the boat, some gentle swishes and others hard, cutting rushes. Then his line straightened with a heavy jerk. He forgot to try to hook the fish; indeed, he had no time. The tarpon came half out of the water, wagged his head, and plumped back. Ken had not hooked the fish, nor had the fish got the bait. So Ken again let out his line.

The next thing which happened was that the boys both had strikes at the same instant. Hal stood up, and as his tarpon leaped it pulled him forward, and he fell into the stern-seat. His reel-handle rattled on the gunwale. The line hissed. Ken leaned back and jerked. His fish did not break water, but he was wonderfully active under the surface. Pepe was jabbering. George was yelling. Hal's fish was tearing the water to shreds. He crossed Ken's fish; the lines fouled, and then slacked. Ken began to wind in. Hal rose to do likewise.

"Gee!" he whispered, with round eyes.

THE LEAPING TARPON

● ● ●

Both lines had been broken. George made light of this incident, and tied on two more leaders and hooks and baited afresh.

"The fish are on the feed, boys. It's a cinch you'll each catch one. Better troll one at a time, unless you can stand for crossed lines."

But Ken and Hal were too eager to catch a tarpon to troll one at a time, so once more they let their lines out. A tarpon took Hal's bait right under the stern of the boat. Hal struck with all his might. This fish came up with a tremendous splash, drenching the boys. His great, gleaming silver sides glistened in the sun. He curved his body and straightened out with a snap like the breaking of a board, and he threw the hook whistling into the air.

Before Hal had baited up, Ken got another strike. This fish made five leaps, one after the other, and upon the last threw the hook like a bullet. As he plunged down, a beautiful rainbow appeared in the misty spray.

"Hal, do you see that rainbow?" cried Ken, quickly. "There's a sight for a fisherman!"

This time in turn, before Ken started to troll, Hal hooked another tarpon. This one was not so large, but he was active. His first rush was a long surge on the surface. He sent the spray in two streaks like a motorboat. Then he sounded.

"Hang on, Hal!" yelled George and Ken in unison.

Hal was bent almost double and his head was bobbing under the strain. He could not hold the drag. The line was whizzing out.

KEN WARD IN THE JUNGLE

• • •

"You got that one hooked," shouted George. "Let go the reel—drop the handle. Let him run."

He complied, and then his fish began a marvelous exhibition of lofty tumbling. He seemed never to stay down at all. Now he shot up, mouth wide, gills spread, eyes wild, and he shook himself like a wet dog. Then he dropped back, and before the boys had time to think where he might be he came up several rods to the right and cracked his gills like pistol shots. He skittered on his tail and stood on his head and dropped flat with a heavy smack. Then he stayed under and began to tug.

"Hang on, now," cried George. "Wind in. Hold him tight. Don't give him an inch unless he jumps."

This was heartbreaking work for Hal. He toiled to keep the line in. He grew red in the face. He dripped with sweat. He panted for breath. But he hung on.

Ken saw how skilfully Pepe managed the boat. The *mozo* seemed to know just which way the fish headed, and always kept the boat straight. Sometimes he rowed back and lent his help to Hal. But this appeared to anger the tarpon, for the line told he was coming to the surface. Then, as Pepe ceased to let him feel the weight of the boat, the tarpon sank again. So the battle went on round and round the great pool. After an hour of it Hal looked ready to drop.

"Land him alone if you can," said Ken. "He's tiring, Hal."

"I'll—land him—or—or bust!" panted Hal.

"Look out, now!" warned George again. "He's coming up. See the line. Be ready to trim the boat if he drops aboard. *Wow!*"

THE LEAPING TARPON

• • •

The tarpon slipped smoothly out of the water and shot right over the bow of the boat. Quick-witted George flung out his hand and threw Hal's rod round in time to save the line from catching. The fish went down, came up wagging his head, and then fell with a sudden splash.

"He's done," yelled George. "Now, Hal, hold him for all you're worth. Not an inch of line!"

Pepe headed the boat for a sandy beach; and Hal, looking as if about to have a stroke of apoplexy, clung desperately to the bending rod. The tarpon rolled and lashed his tail, but his power was mostly gone. Gradually he ceased to roll, until by the time Pepe reached shore he was sliding wearily through the water, his silvery side glittering in the light.

The boat grated on the sand. Pepe leaped out. Then he grasped Hal's line, slipped his hands down to the long wire leader, and with a quick, powerful pull slid the tarpon out upon the beach.

"Oh-h!" gasped Hal, with glistening eyes. "Oh-h! Ken, just look!"

"I'm looking, son, and don't you forget it."

The tarpon lay inert, a beautiful silver-scaled creature that looked as if he had just come from a bath of melted opals. The great dark eyes were fixed and staring, the tail moved feebly, the long dorsal fin quivered.

He measured five feet six inches in length, which was one inch more than Hal's height.

"Ken, the boys back home will never believe I caught him," said Hal, in distress.

● ● ●

"Take his picture to prove it," replied Ken.

Hal photographed his catch. Pepe took out the hook, showing, as he did so, the great iron-like plates in the mouth of the fish.

"No wonder it's hard to hook them," said Ken.

Hal certainly wanted his beautiful fish to go back, free and little hurt, to the river. But also he wanted him for a specimen. Hal deliberated. Evidently he was considering the labor of skinning such a huge fish and the difficulty of preserving and packing the hide.

"Say, Hal, wouldn't you like to see me hook one?" queried Ken, patiently.

That brought Hal to his senses.

"Sure, Ken, old man, I want you to catch one—a big one—bigger than mine," replied Hal, and restored the fish to the water.

They all watched the liberated tarpon swim wearily off and slip down under the water.

"He'll have something to tell the rest, won't he?" said George.

In a few minutes the boat was again in the center of the great pool among the rolling tarpon. Ken had a strike immediately. He missed. Then he tried again. And in a short space of time he saw five tarpon in the air, one after the other, and not one did he hook securely. He got six leaps out of one, however, and that was almost as good as landing him.

"There're some whales here," said George.

"Grande savalo," added Pepe, and he rowed over to where a huge fish was rolling.

"Oh, I don't want to hook the biggest one first," protested Ken.

THE LEAPING TARPON

• • •

Pepe rowed to and fro. The boys were busy trying to see the rolling tarpon. There would be a souse on one side, then a splash on the other, then a thump behind. What with trying to locate all these fish and still keep an eye on Ken's line the boys almost dislocated their necks.

Then, quick as a flash, Ken had a strike that pulled him out of his seat to his knees. He could not jerk. His line was like a wire. It began to rise. With all his strength he held on. The water broke in a hollow, slow roar, and a huge humpbacked tarpon seemed to be climbing into the air. But he did not get all the way out, and he plunged back with a thunderous crash. He made as much noise as if a horse had fallen off a bridge.

The handle of the reel slipped out of Ken's grasp, and it was well. The tarpon made a long, wonderful run and showed on the surface a hundred yards from the boat. He was irresistibly powerful. Ken was astounded and thrilled at his strength and speed. There, far away from the boat, the tarpon leaped magnificently, clearing the water, and then went down. He did not come up again.

"Ken, he's a whale," said George. "I believe he's well hooked. He won't jump any more. And you've got a job on your hands."

"I want him to jump."

"The big ones seldom break water after the first rush or so."

"Ken, it's coming to you with that fellow," said Hal. "My left arm is paralyzed. Honestly, I can pinch it and not feel the pain."

217

KEN WARD IN THE JUNGLE

● ● ●

Pepe worked the boat closer and Ken reeled in yard after yard of line. The tarpon was headed downstream, and he kept up a steady, strong strain.

"Let him tow the boat," said George. "Hold the drag, Ken. Let him tow the boat."

"What!" exclaimed Ken, in amaze.

"Oh, he'll do it, all right."

And so it proved. Ken's tarpon, once headed with the current, did not turn, and he towed the boat.

"This is a new way for me to tire out a fish," said Ken. "What do you think of it, Hal?"

Hal's eyes glistened.

"This is fishing. Ken, did you see him when he came up?"

"Not very clearly. I had buck-fever. You know how a grouse looks when he flushes right under your feet—a kind of brown blur. Well, this was the same, only silver."

At the end of what Ken judged to be a mile the tarpon was still going. At the end of the second mile he was tired. And three miles down the river from where the fish was hooked Pepe beached the boat on a sandbar and hauled ashore a tarpon six feet ten inches long.

Here Ken echoed Hal's panting gasp of wonder and exultation. As he sat down on the boat to rest he had no feeling in his left arm, and little in his right. His knuckles were skinned and bloody. No game of baseball he had ever pitched had taken his strength like the conquest of this magnificent fish.

"Hal, we'll have some more of this fishing when we get to Tampico," said Ken. "Why, this beats hunting.

THE LEAPING TARPON

● ● ●

You have the sport, and you needn't kill anything. This tarpon isn't hurt."

So Ken photographed his prize and measured him, and, taking a last lingering glance at the great green back, the silver-bronze sides, the foot-wide flukes of the tail, at the whole quivering, fire-tinted length, he slid the tarpon back into the river.

22

Stricken Down

●

Much as Ken would have liked to go back to that pool, he did not think of it twice. And as soon as the excitement had subsided and the journey was resumed, George and Hal, and Pepe, too, settled down into a silent weariness that made Ken anxious.

During the afternoon Ken saw Pepe slowly droop lower and lower at the oars till the time came when he could scarcely lift them to make a stroke. And when Ken relieved him of them, Pepe fell like a log in the boat.

George slept. Hal seemed to be fighting stupor. Pepe lay motionless on his seat. They were all going down with the fever, that Ken knew, and it took all his courage to face the situation. It warmed his heart to see how Hal was trying to bear up under a languor that must

● ● ●

have been well-nigh impossible to resist. At last Hal said:

"Ken, let me row." He would not admit that he was sick.

Ken thought it would do Hal no harm to work. But Ken did not want to lose time. So he hit upon a plan that pleased him. There was an extra pair of oars in the boat. Ken fashioned rude pegs from a stick and drove these down into the cleat inside the gunwales. With stout rope he tied the oars to the pegs, which answered fairly well as oarlocks. Then they had a double set of oars going, and made much better time.

George woke and declared that he must take a turn at the oars. So Ken let him row, too, and rested himself. He had a grim foreboding that he would need all his strength.

The succeeding few hours before sunset George and Hal more than made up for all their delinquencies of the past. At first it was not very hard for them to row; but soon they began to weary, then weaken. Neither one, however, would give up. Ken let them row, knowing that it was good for them. Slower and slower grew George's strokes. There were times when he jerked up spasmodically and made an effort, only to weaken again. At last, with a groan he dropped the oars. Ken had to lift him back into the bow.

Hal was not so sick as George, and therefore not so weak. He lasted longer. Ken had seen the lad stick to many a hard job, but never as he did to this one. Hal was making good his promise. There were times when his breath came in whistles. He would stop and pant awhile, then row on. Ken pretended he did not notice.

KEN WARD IN THE JUNGLE

• • •

But he had never been so proud of his brother nor loved him so well.

"Ken, old man," said Hal, presently. "I was— wrong—about the water. I ought to have obeyed you. I—I'm pretty sick."

What a confession for Hal Ward!

Ken turned in time to see Hal vomit over the gun-wale.

"It's pretty tough, Hal," said Ken, as he reached out to hold his brother's head, "but you're game. I'm so glad to see that."

Whereupon Hal went back to his oars and stayed till he dropped. Ken lifted him and laid him beside George.

Ken rowed on with his eyes ever in search of a camping-site. But there was no place to camp. The muddy banks were too narrow at the bottom, too marshy and filthy. And they were too steep to climb to the top.

The sun set. Twilight fell. Darkness came on, and still Ken rowed down the river. At last he decided to make a night of it at the oars. He preferred to risk the dangers of the river at night rather than spend miserable hours in the mud. Rousing the boys, he forced them to swallow a little cold rice and some more quinine. Then he covered them with blankets, and had scarce completed the task when they were deep in slumber.

Then the strange, dense tropical night settled down upon Ken. The oars were almost noiseless, and the water gurgled softly from the bow. Overhead the expanse was dark blue, with a few palpitating stars. The river was shrouded in gray gloom, and the banks were lost in black obscurity. Great fireflies emphasized the darkness.

STRICKEN DOWN

● ● ●

He trusted a good deal to luck in the matter of going right; yet he kept his ear keen for the sound of quickening current, and turned every few strokes to peer sharply into the gloom. He seemed to have little sense of peril, for, though he hit submerged logs and stranded on bars, he kept on unmindful, and by and by lost what anxiety he had felt. The strange wildness of the river at night, the gray, veiled space into which he rowed unheeding began to work upon his mind.

That was a night to remember—a night of sounds and smells, of the feeling of the cool mist, the sight of long, dark forest-line and a golden moon half hidden by clouds. Prominent among these was the trill of river frogs. The trill of a northern frog was music, but that of these great, silver-throated jungle frogs was more than music. Close at hand one would thrill Ken with mellow, rich notes; and then from far would come the answer, a sweet, high tenor, wilder than any other wilderness sound, long sustained, dying away till he held his breath to listen.

So the hours passed, and the moon went down into the weird shadows, and the Southern Cross rose pale and wonderful.

Gradually the stars vanished in a kind of brightening gray, and dawn was at hand. Ken felt weary for sleep, and his arms and back ached. Morning came, with its steely light on the river, the rolling and melting of vapors, the flight of ducks and call of birds. The rosy sun brought no cheer.

Ken beached the boat on a sand-bar. While he was building a fire George raised his head and groaned. But neither Pepe nor Hal moved. Ken cooked rice and boiled cocoa, which he choked down. He opened a can of fruit and found that most welcome. Then he lifted George's head, shook him, roused him, and held him, and made him eat and drink. Nor did he neglect to put a liberal dose of quinine in the food. Pepe was easily managed, but poor Hal was almost unable to swallow. Something terribly grim mingled with a strong, passionate thrill as Ken looked at Hal's haggard face. Then Ken Ward knew how much he could stand, what work he could do to get his brother out of the jungle.

He covered the boys again and pushed out the boat. At the moment he felt a strength that he had never felt before. There was a good, swift current in the river, and Ken was at great pains to keep in it. The channel ran from one side of the river to the other. Many times Ken stranded on sandy shoals and had to stand up and pole the boat into deeper water. This was work that required all his attention. It required more than patience. But as he rowed and poled and drifted he studied the shallow ripples and learned to avoid the places where the boat would not float.

There were stretches of river where the water was comparatively deep, and along these he rested and watched the shores as he drifted by. He saw no Indian huts that morning. The jungle loomed high and dark, a matted gray wall. The heat made the river glare and smoke. Then where the current quickened he rowed steadily and easily, husbanding his strength.

More than all else, even the ravings of Hal in fever, the thing that wore on Ken and made him gloomy was the mourning of the turtle-doves. As there had been thousands of these beautiful birds along the Santa Rosa

STRICKEN DOWN

● ● ●

River, so there were millions along the Panuco. Trees were blue with doves. There was an incessant soft, sad moaning. He fought his nervous, sensitive imaginings. And for a time he would conquer the sense of some sad omen sung by the doves. Then the monotony, the endless sweet "coo-ooo-ooo," seemed to drown him in melancholy sound. There were three distinct tones—a moan, swelling to full ring, and dying away: "Coo-*ooo-ooo*—coo-*ooo*-ooo."

All the afternoon the mourning, haunting song filled Ken Ward's ears. And when the sun set and night came, with relief to his tortured ear but not to mind, Ken kept on without a stop.

The day had slipped behind Ken with the miles, and now it was again dark. It seemed that he had little sense of time. But his faculties of sight and hearing were singularly acute. Otherwise his mind was like the weird gloom in which he was drifting.

Before the stars came out the blackness was as thick as pitch. He could not see a yard ahead. He backed the boat stern first downstream and listened for the soft murmur of ripples on shoals. He avoided these by hearing alone. Occasionally a huge, dark pile of driftwood barred his passage, and he would have to go round it. Snags loomed up specter-like in his path, seemingly to reach for him with long, gaunt arms. Sometimes he drifted upon sand-bars, from which he would patiently pole the boat.

When the heavy dew began to fall he put on his waterproof coat. The night grew chill. Then the stars shone out. This lightened the river. Yet everywhere were shad-

• • •

ows. Besides, clouds of mist hung low, in places obscuring the stars.

Ken turned the boat bow first downstream and rowed with slow, even strokes. He no longer felt tired. He seemed to have the strength of a giant. He fancied that with one great heave he could lift the boat out of the water or break the oars. From time to time he ceased to row, and, turning his head, he looked and listened. The river had numerous bends, and it was difficult for Ken to keep in the middle channel. He managed pretty well to keep right by watching the dark shoreline where it met the deep blue sky. In the bends the deepest water ran close to the shore of the outside curve. And under these high banks and the leaning cypresses shadows were thicker and blacker than in the earlier night. There was mystery in them that Ken felt.

The sounds he heard when he stopped during these cautious resting intervals were the splashes of fish breaking water, the low hum of insects, and the trill of frogs. The mourning of the doves during daylight had haunted him, and now he felt the same sensation at this long-sustained, exquisitely sweet trill. It pierced him, racked him, and at last, from sheer exhaustion of his sensibilities, he seemed not to hear it any more, but to have it in his brain.

The moon rose behind the left-hand jungle wall, silvered half of the river and the opposite line of cypresses, then hid under clouds.

Suddenly, near or far away, down the river Ken saw a wavering light. It was too large for a firefly, and too steady. He took it for a Jack-o'-lantern. And for a while it enhanced the unreality, the ghostliness of the river.

STRICKEN DOWN

● ● ●

But it was the means of bringing Ken out of his dreamy gloom. It made him think. The light was moving. It was too wavering for a Jack-o'-lantern. It was coming upstream. It grew larger.

Then, as suddenly as it had appeared, it vanished. Ken lost sight of it under a deep shadow of overhanging shore. As he reached a point opposite to where it disappeared he thought he heard a voice. But he could not be sure. He did not trust his ears. The incident, however, gave him a chill. What a lonesome ride! He was alone on that unknown river with three sick boys in the boat. Their lives depended upon his care, his strength, his skill, his sight and hearing. And the realization, striking him afresh, steeled his arms again and his spirit.

The night wore on. The moon disappeared entirely. The mists hung low like dim sheets along the water. Ken was wringing wet with dew. Long periods of rowing he broke with short intervals of drifting, when he rested at the oars.

Then drowsiness attacked him. For hours it seemed he fought it off. But at length it grew overpowering. Only hard rowing would keep him awake. And, as he wanted to reserve his strength, he did not dare exert himself violently. He could not keep his eyes open. Time after time he found himself rowing when he was half asleep. The boat drifted against a log and stopped. Ken drooped over his oars and slept, and yet he seemed not altogether to lose consciousness. He roused again to row on.

It occurred to him presently that he might let the boat drift and take naps between whiles. When he drifted against a log or a sand-bar the jar would awaken him.

KEN WARD IN THE JUNGLE

• • •

The current was sluggish. There seemed to be no danger whatever. He must try to keep his strength. A little sleep would refresh him. So he reasoned, and fell asleep over the oars.

Sooner or later—he never knew how long after he had fallen asleep—a little jar awakened him. Then the gurgle and murmur of water near him and the rush and roar of a swift current farther off made him look up with a violent start. All about him was wide, gray gloom. Yet he could see the dark, glancing gleam of the water. Movement of the oars told him the boat was fast on a sand-bar. That relieved him, for he was not drifting at the moment into the swift current he heard. Ken peered keenly into the gloom. Gradually he made out a long, dark line running diagonally ahead of him and toward the right-hand shore. It could not be an island or a sand-bar or a shoreline. It could not be piles of driftwood. There was a strange regularity in the dark upheavals of this looming object. Ken studied it. He studied the black, glancing water. Whatever the line was, it appeared to shunt the current over to the right, whence came the low rush and roar.

Altogether it was a wild, strange place. Ken felt a fear of something he could not name. It was the river—the night—the loneliness—the unknown about him and before him.

Suddenly he saw a dull, red light far down the river. He stiffened in his seat. Then he saw another red light. They were like two red eyes. Ken shook himself to see if it was a nightmare. No, the boat was there; the current was there; the boys were there, dark and silent under their blankets. This was no dream. Ken's fancy

● ● ●

conjured up some red-eyed river demon come to destroy him and his charges. He scorned the fancy, laughed at it. But, all the same, in that dark, weird place, with the murmuring of notes in his ears and with those strange red eyes glowing in the distance, he could not help what his emotions made the truth. He was freezing to the marrow, writhing in a clammy sweat when a low "chug-chug-chug" enlightened him. The red eyes were those of a steamboat.

A steamboat on the wild Panuco! Ken scarcely believed his own judgment. Then he remembered that George said there were a couple of boats plying up and down the lower Panuco, mostly transporting timber and cattle. Besides, he had proof of his judgment in the long, dark line that had so puzzled him—it was a breakwater. It turned the current to the left, where there evidently was a channel.

The great, red eyes gleamed closer, the "chug-chug-chug" sounded louder. Then another sound amazed Ken—a man's voice crying out steadily and monotonously.

Ken wanted to rouse the boys and Pepe, but he refrained. It was best for them to sleep. How surprised they would be when he told them about the boat that passed in the night! Ken now clearly heard the splashing of paddles, the chug of machinery, and the man's voice. He was singsonging: "Dos y media, dos y media, dos y media."

Ken understood a little Mexican, and this strange cry became clear to him. The man was taking soundings with a lead and crying out to the pilot. *Dos y media* meant two and a half feet of water. Then the steamboat loomed black in the gray gloom. It was pushing a low, flat barge. Ken could not see the man taking soundings, but he heard him and knew he was on the front end of the barge. The boat passed at fair speed, and it cheered Ken. For he certainly ought to be able to take a rowboat where a steamboat had passed. And, besides, he must be getting somewhere near the little village of Panuco.

He poled off the bar and along the break-water to the channel. It was narrow and swift. He wondered how the pilot of the steamboat had navigated in the gloom. He slipped downstream, presently to find himself once more in a wide river. Refreshed by his sleep and encouraged by the meeting with the steamboat, Ken settled down to steady rowing.

The stars paled, the mist thickened, fog obscured the water and shore; then all turned gray, lightened, and dawn broke. The sun burst out. Ken saw thatched huts high on the banks and occasionally natives. This encouraged him all the more.

He was not hungry, but he was sick for a drink. He had to fight himself to keep from drinking the dirty river-water. How different it was here from the clear green of the upper Santa Rosa! Ken would have given his best gun for one juicy orange. George was restless and rolling about, calling for water; Hal lay in slumber or stupor; and Pepe sat up. He was a sick-looking fellow, but he was better; and that cheered Ken as nothing yet had.

Ken beached the boat on a sandy shore, and once again forced down a little rice and cocoa. Pepe would not eat, yet he drank a little. George was burning up with fever, and drank a full cup. Hal did not stir, and Ken thought it best to let him lie.

As Ken resumed the journey the next thing to attract his attention was a long canoe moored below one of the thatched huts. This afforded him great satisfaction. At least he had passed the jungle wilderness, where there was nothing that even suggested civilization. In the next few miles he noticed several canoes and as many natives. Then he passed a canoe that was paddled by two half-naked bronze Indians. Pepe hailed them, but either they were too unfriendly to reply or they did not understand him.

Some distance below Pepe espied a banana grove, and he motioned Ken to row ashore. Ken did so with pleasure at the thought of getting some fresh fruit. There was a canoe moored to the roots of a tree and a path leading up the steep bank. Pepe got out and laboriously toiled up the bare path. He was gone a good while.

Presently Ken heard shouts, then the bang of a lightly loaded gun, then yells from Pepe.

"What on earth!" cried Ken, looking up in affright.

Pepe appeared with his arms full of red bananas. He jumped and staggered down the path and almost fell into the boat. But he hung on to the bananas.

"Santa Maria!" gasped Pepe, pointing to little bloody spots on the calf of his leg.

"Pepe, you've been shot!" ejaculated Ken. "You stole the fruit—somebody shot you!"

Pepe howled his affirmative. Ken was angry at himself, angrier at Pepe, and angriest at the native who had done the shooting. With a strong shove Ken put the boat

● ● ●

out and then rowed hard downstream. As he rounded a bend a hundred yards below he saw three natives come tumbling down the path. They had a gun. They leaped into the canoe. They meant pursuit.

"Say, but this is a pretty kettle of fish!" muttered Ken, and he bent to the oars.

Of course Pepe had been in the wrong. He should have paid for the bananas or asked for them. All the same, Ken was not in any humor to be fooled with by excitable natives. He had a sick brother in the boat and meant to get that lad out of the jungle as quickly as will and strength could do it. He certainly did not intend to be stopped by a few miserable Indians angry over the loss of a few bananas. If it had not been for the gun, Ken would have stopped long enough to pay for the fruit. But he could not risk it now. So he pulled a strong stroke downstream.

The worst of the matter developed when Pepe peeled one of the bananas. It was too green to eat.

Presently the native canoe hove in sight round the bend. All three men were paddling. They made the long craft fly through the water. Ken saw instantly that they would overhaul him in a long race, and this added to his resentment. Pepe looked back and jabbered and shook his brawny fists at the natives. Ken was glad to see that the long stretch of river below did not show a canoe or hut along the banks. He preferred to be overhauled, if he had to be, in a rather lonely spot.

It was wonderful how those natives propelled that log canoe. And when one of the three dropped his paddle to pick up the gun, the speed of the canoe seemed not to diminish. They knew the channels, and so gained on

STRICKEN DOWN

● ● ●

Ken. He had to pick the best he could choose at short notice, and sometimes he chose poorly.

Two miles or more below the bend the natives with the gun deliberately fired, presumably at Pepe. The shot scattered and skipped along the water and did not come near the boat. Nevertheless, as the canoe was gaining and the crazy native was reloading, Ken saw he would soon be within range. Something had to be done.

Ken wondered if he could not frighten those natives. They had probably never heard the quick reports of a repeating rifle, let alone the stinging cracks of an automatic. Ken decided it would be worth trying. But he must have a chance to get the gun out of its case and load it.

That chance came presently. The natives, in paddling diagonally across a narrow channel, ran aground in the sand. They were fast for only a few moments, but in that time Ken had got out the little rifle and loaded it.

Pepe's dark face turned a dirty white, and his eyes dilated. He imagined Ken was going to kill some of his countrymen. But Pepe never murmured. He rubbed the place in his leg where he had been shot, and looked back.

Ken rowed on, now leisurely. There was a hot anger within him, but he had it in control. He knew what he was about. Again the native fired, and again his range was short. The distance was perhaps two hundred yards.

Ken waited until the canoe, in crossing one of the many narrow places, was broadside toward him. Then he raised the automatic. There were at least ten feet in the middle of the canoe where it was safe for him to hit without harm to the natives. And there he aimed. The motion of his boat made it rather hard to keep the sights right. He was cool, careful; he aimed low, between gunwale and the water, and steadily he pulled the trigger—once, twice, three times, four, five.

The steel-jacketed bullets "spoued" on the water and "cracked" into the canoe. They evidently split both gunwales low down at the water-line. The yelling, terror-stricken natives plunged about, and what with their actions and the great split in the middle the canoe filled and sank. The natives were not over their depth; that was plainly evident. Moreover, it was equally evident that they dared not wade in the quicksand. So they swam to the shallower water, and there, like huge turtles, floundered toward the shore.

23

Out of the Jungle

●

Before the natives had reached the shore they were hidden from Ken's sight by leaning cypress trees. Ken, however, had no fear for their safety. He was sorry to cause the Indians' loss of a gun and a canoe; nevertheless, he was not far from echoing Pepe's repeated: "Bueno! Bueno! Bueno!"

Upon examination Ken found two little bloody holes in the muscles of Pepe's leg. A single shot had passed through. Ken bathed the wounds with an antiseptic lotion and bound them with clean bandages.

Pepe appeared to be pretty weak, so Ken did not ask him to take the oars. Then, pulling with long, steady strokes, Ken set out to put a long stretch between him and the angry natives. The current was swift, and Ken made five miles or more an hour. He kept that pace for three hours without a rest. And then he gave out. It

• • •

seemed that all at once he weakened. His back bore an immense burden. His arms were lead, and his hands were useless. There was an occasional mist or veil before his sight. He was wet, hot, breathless, numb. But he knew he was safe from pursuit. So he rested and let the boat drift.

George sat up, green in the face, a most miserable-looking boy. But that he could sit up at all was hopeful.

"Oh, my head!" he moaned. "Is there anything I can drink? My mouth is dry—pasted shut."

Ken had two lemons he had been saving. He cut one in halves and divided it between Pepe and George. The relief the sour lemon afforded both showed Ken how wise he had been to save the lemons. Then he roused Hal, and, lifting the lad's head, made him drink a little of the juice. Hal was a sick boy, too weak to sit up without help.

"Don't—you worry—Ken," he said. "I'm going—to be—all right."

Hal was still fighting.

Ken readjusted the palm-leaf shelter over the boys so as to shade them effectually from the hot sun, and then he went back to the oars.

As he tried once more to row, Ken was reminded of the terrible lassitude that had overtaken him the day he had made the six-hour climb out of the Grand Cañon. The sensation now was worse, but Ken had others, depending upon his exertions, and that spurred him to the effort which otherwise would have been impossible.

It was really not rowing that Ken accomplished. It was a weary puttering with oars he could not lift, handles he could not hold. At best he managed to guide the

● ● ●

boat into the swiftest channels. Whenever he felt that he was just about to collapse, he would look at Hal's pale face. That would revive him. So the hot hours dragged by.

They came, after several miles, upon more huts and natives. And farther down they met canoes on the river. Pepe interrogated the natives. According to George, who listened, Panuco was far, far away, many kilometers. This was most disheartening. Another native said the village was just round the next bend. This was most happy information. But it turned out to be a lie. There was no village round any particular bend—nothing save bare banks for miles. The stretches of the river were long, and bends far apart.

Ken fell asleep. When he awoke he found Pepe at the oars. Watching him, Ken fancied he was recovering, and was overjoyed.

About four o'clock in the afternoon Pepe rowed ashore and beached the boat at the foot of a trail leading up to a large bamboo and thatch hut. This time Ken thought it well to accompany Pepe. And as he climbed the path he found his legs stiffer and shakier than ever before.

Ken saw a cleared space in which were several commodious huts, gardens, and flowers. There was a grassy yard in which little naked children were playing with tame deer and tiger-cats. Parrots were screeching, and other tame birds fluttered about. It appeared a real paradise to Ken.

Two very kindly disposed and wondering native women made them welcome. Then Ken and Pepe went down to the boat and carried Hal up, and went back for George.

It developed that the native women knew just what to do for the fever-stricken boys. They made some kind of a native drink for them, and after that gave them hot milk and chicken and rice soup. George improved rapidly, and Hal brightened a little and showed signs of gathering strength.

Ken could not eat until he had something to quench his thirst. Upon inquiring, Pepe found that the natives used the river-water. Ken could not drink that. Then Pepe pointed out an orange tree, and Ken made a dive for it. The ground was littered with oranges. Collecting an armful, Ken sat under the tree and with wild haste began to squeeze the juice into his mouth. Never had anything before tasted so cool, so sweet, so life-giving! He felt a cool, wet sensation steal all through his body. He never knew till that moment how really wonderful and precious an orange could be. He thought that as he would hate mourning turtle-doves all the rest of his life, so he would love the sight and smell and taste of oranges. And he demolished twenty-two before he satisfied his almost insatiable thirst. After that the chicken and rice made him feel like a new boy.

Then Ken made beds under a kind of porch, and he lay down in one, stretched out languidly and gratefully, as if he never intended to move again, and his eyes seemed to be glued shut.

When he awoke the sun was shining in his face. When he had gone to bed it had been shining at his back. He consulted his watch. He had slept seventeen hours.

OUT OF THE JUNGLE

• • •

When he got up and found Pepe as well as before he had been taken with the fever and George on his feet and Hal awake and actually smiling, Ken experienced a sensation of unutterable thankfulness. A terrible burden slipped from his shoulders. For a moment he felt a dimming of his eyes and a lump in his throat.

"How about you, Ken, old man?" inquired Hal, with a hint of his usual spirit.

"Wal, youngster, I reckon fer a man who's been through some right pert happenin's, I'm in tol'able shape," drawled Ken.

"I'll bet two dollars you've been up against it," declared Hal, solemnly.

Then, as they sat to an appetizing breakfast, Ken gave them a brief account of the incidents of the two days and two nights when they were too ill to know anything.

It was a question whether George's voluble eulogy of Ken's feat or Hal's silent, bright-eyed pride in his brother was the greater compliment.

Finally Hal said: "Won't that tickle Jim Williams when we tell him how you split up the Indians' canoe and spilled them into the river?"

Then Ken conceived the idea of climbing into the giant ceiba that stood high on the edge of the bluff. It was hard work, but he accomplished it, and from a fork in the top-most branches he looked out. That was a warm, rich, wonderful scene. Ken felt that he would never forget it. His interest now, however, was not so much in its beauty and wildness. His keen eye followed the river as it wound away into the jungle, and when he could no longer see the bright ribbon of water he followed its

• • •

course by the line of magnificent trees. It was possible to trace the meandering course of the river clear to the rise of the mountains, dim and blue in the distance. And from here Ken made more observations and notes.

As he went over in his mind the map and notes and report he had prepared he felt that he had made good. He had explored and mapped more than a hundred miles of wild jungle river. He felt confident that he had earned the trip to England and the German forests. He might win a hunting trip on the vast uplands of British East Africa. But he felt also that the reward of his uncle's and his father's pride would be more to him. That was a great moment for Ken Ward. And there was yet much more that he could do to make this exploring trip a success.

When he joined the others he found that Pepe had learned that the village of Panuco was distant a day or a night by canoe. How many miles or kilometers Pepe could not learn. Ken decided it would be best to go on at once. It was not easy to leave that pleasant place, with its music of parrots and other birds, and the tiger-cats that played like kittens, and the deer that ate from the hand. The women would accept no pay, so Ken made them presents.

Once more embarked, Ken found his mood reverting to that of the last forty-eight hours. He could not keep cheerful. The river was dirty and the smell sickening. The sun was like the open door of a furnace. And Ken soon discovered he was tired, utterly tired.

That day was a repetition of the one before, hotter, wearier, and the stretches of river were longer, and the natives met in canoes were stolidly ignorant of distance.

OUT OF THE JUNGLE

• • •

The mourning of turtle-doves almost drove Ken wild. There were miles and miles of willows, and every tree was full of melancholy doves. At dusk the boys halted on a sand-bar, too tired to cook a dinner, and sprawled in the warm sand to sleep like logs.

In the morning they brightened up a little, for surely just around the bend they would come to Panuco. Pepe rowed faithfully on, and bend after bend lured Ken with deceit. He was filled with weariness and disgust, so tired he could hardly lift his hand, so sleepy he could scarcely keep his eyes open. He hated the wide, glassy stretches of river and the muddy banks and dusty cattle.

At noon they came unexpectedly upon a cluster of thatched huts, to find that they made up the village of Panuco. Ken was sick, for he had expected a little town where they could get some drinking water and hire a launch to speed them down to Tampico. This appeared little more than the other places he had passed, and he climbed up the bank wearily, thinking of the long fifty miles still to go.

But Panuco was bigger and better than it looked from the river. The boys found a clean, comfortable inn, where they dined well, and learned to their joy that a coach left in an hour for Tamos to meet the five-o'clock train to Tampico.

They hired a *mozo* to row the boat to Tampico and, carrying the lighter things, boarded the coach, and, behind six mules, were soon bowling over a good level road.

It was here that the spirit of Ken's mood again changed, and somehow seemed subtly conveyed to the others. The gloom faded away as Ken had seen the

• • •

mist-clouds dissolve in the morning sunlight. It was the end of another wild trip. Hal was ill, but a rest and proper care would soon bring him around. Ken had some trophies and pictures, but he also had memories. And he believed he had acquired an accurate knowledge of the jungle and its wild nature, and he had mapped the river from Micas Falls to Panuco.

"Well, it certainly *did come* to us, didn't it?" asked George, naïvely, for the hundredth time. "Didn't I tell you? By gosh, I can't remember what did come off. But we had a dandy time."

"Great!" replied Ken. "I had more than I wanted. I'll never spring another stunt like this one!"

Hal gazed smilingly at his brother.

"Bah! Ken Ward, bring on your next old trip!"

Which proved decidedly that Hal was getting better and that he alone understood his brother.

Pepe listened and rubbed his big hands, and there was a light in his dark eyes.

Ken laughed. It was good to feel happy just then; it was enough to feel safe and glad in the present, with responsibility removed, without a thought of the future.

Yet, when some miles across country he saw the little town of Tamos shining red-roofed against the sky, he came into his own again. The old calling, haunting love of wild places and wild nature returned, and with dreamy eyes he looked out. He saw the same beauty and life and wildness. Beyond the glimmering lagoons stretched the dim, dark jungle. A flock of flamingoes showed pink across the water. Ducks dotted the weedy marshes. And low down on the rosy horizon a long curved line of wild geese sailed into the sunset.

OUT OF THE JUNGLE
● ● ●

When the boys arrived at Tampico and George had secured comfortable lodgings for them, the first thing Ken did was to put Hal to bed. It required main strength to do this. Ken was not taking any chances with tropical fever, and he sent for a doctor.

It was not clear whether the faces Hal made were at the little dried-up doctor or at the medicine he administered. However, it was very clear that Hal made fun of him and grew bolder the more he believed the man could not understand English.

Ken liked the silent, kindly physician, and remonstrated with Hal, and often, just to keep Hal's mind occupied, he would talk of the university and baseball, topics that were absorbing to the boy.

And one day, as the doctor was leaving, he turned to Ken with a twinkle in his eyes and said in perfect English: "I won't need to come any more."

Hal's jaw began to drop.

"Your brother is all right," went on the doctor. "But he's a fresh kid, and he'll never make the Wayne Varsity—or a good explorer, either—till he gets over that freshness. I'm a Wayne man myself. Class of '82. Good day, boys."

Ken Ward was astounded. "By George! What do you think of that? He's a Wayne med. I'll have to look him up. And, Hal, he was just right about you."

Hal looked extremely crestfallen and remorseful.

"I'm always getting jars."

It took a whole day for him to recover his usual spirits.

Ken had promptly sent the specimens and his notes to

243

KEN WARD IN THE JUNGLE

● ● ●

his uncle, and as the days passed the boys began to look anxiously for some news. In ten days Hal was as well as ever, and then the boys had such sport with the tarpon and big sharks and alligator-gars that they almost forgot about the rewards they had striven so hard for and hoped to win. But finally, when the mail arrived from home, they were at once happy and fearful. George was with them that evening, and shared their excitement and suspense. Hal's letters were from his mother and his sister, and they were read first. Judge Ward's letter to Ken was fatherly and solicitous, but brief. He gave the boys six more weeks, cautioned them to be sensible and to profit by their opportunity, and he enclosed a bank draft. Not a word about rewards!

Ken's fingers trembled a little as he tore open the uncle's letter. He read it aloud:

DEAR KEN,—Congratulations! You've done well. You win the trip to Africa. Hal's work also was good—several specimens accepted by the Smithsonian. I'll back you for the Yucatan trip. Will send letters to the American consul at Progreso, and arrange for you to meet the Austrian archeologist Maler, who I hope will take you in hand.

I want you to make a study of some of the ruins of Yucatan, which I believe are as wonderful as any in Egypt. I advise you to make this trip short and to the point, for there are indications of coming revolution throughout Mexico.

With best wishes,

UNCLE G.

OUT OF THE JUNGLE

•   •   •

The old varsity cheer rang out from Ken, and Hal began a war dance. Then both boys pounced upon George, and for a few moments made life miserable for him.

"And I can't go with you!" he exclaimed sorrowfully.

Both Ken and Hal shared his disappointment. But presently George brightened up. The smile came back which he always wore when prophesying the uncertain adventures of the future.

"Well, anyway, I'll be safe home. And you fellows! You'll be getting yours when you're lost in the wilderness of Yucatan!"